Jeanne Crews Taylor
Best Wishes

The Final Stretch

Jeanne Crews Taylor

authorHOUSE®

AuthorHouse™
1663 Liberty Drive
Bloomington, IN 47403
www.authorhouse.com
Phone: 1-800-839-8640

First published by AuthorHouse 4/15/2011

ISBN: 978-1-4567-2753-6 (e)
ISBN: 978-1-4567-2754-3 (sc)

Printed in the United States of America

Any people depicted in stock imagery provided by Thinkstock are models, and such images are being used for illustrative purposes only. Certain stock imagery © Thinkstock.

This book is printed on acid-free paper.

Many thanks to the Ted Nolands of Beggs, Oklahoma for time spent observing horses on their ranch. Also, my thanks to Ann Stewart of Advantage Services for her faithful assistance in manuscript preps and of course to my family who is a constant support.

CHAPTER 1

THE ER AT WEST Hills Hospital was calm Wednesday evening; fewer wrecks and shootings. Folks probably Christmas shopping or at church; Oklahoma folks attended mid-week services. The Christmas season always brought a hurry and bustle to the malls, too, which reminded Retta Roark that she still had shopping to do. She adjusted a Dextrose tube in case it was needed while there was time to kill and flipped on a small radio on a nearby table. Oklahoma City was undergoing a severe winter storm. Suddenly, there was more—a special bulletin! "External Code," a dispatch announced. She dropped the tube to listen. EMTs were announcing an airline catastrophe at the airport. Mercer Airlines flight 960 from Pittsburgh had skidded on landing, flipped, and exploded. Captain Burgress wrestled to correct the yaw but lost control under the worst weather conditions in decades!

Retta pushed the intercom to prepare for the worst—call in off-duty staff, both physicians and nurses, alert both the trauma and burn centers; certainly the blood bank needed to prepare blood and plasma expanders, and X-ray might need additional staff. Just what kind of injuries might come in, it was hard to predict. With that kind of explosion, most passengers probably died instantly—cremated in mid-air. Terrible, Retta thought, when the radio announcer stated that victims and luggage were spewed into the air over a wide area. "My gosh, oh, my gosh!" she muttered as she set up a triage where the wounded could be categorized as to the severity of their injuries. It was her first disaster at West Hills since she began her nursing career; she wondered whether she'd chosen the wrong profession.

Within minutes, the ER turned into a mixing bowl of confusion; blood spurting uncontrollably, injured groaning and screaming, loud gasps for breath, and faces already ashen and cold. One young man, probably twenty, had lost a leg. With only scraps of clothing dangling from his midsection, he was bleeding profusely. "Over here," Retta yelled, rushing to his side.

A fortyish-looking man had a long laceration on his right shoulder and was bleeding from his mouth and ears. His deep groans carried over the entire west wing of the hospital, names such as *Claire, Persia*, whoever they were. Retta steadied herself; she felt faint. But when an older woman came in with her entire abdomen gaping so that most of her internal organs showed, Retta closed her eyes, totally devastated. Oh, God, too much, she thought… can't take this!

"Take the woman back to the trauma center," Dr. Spraggins yelled when he saw three teenage girls brought in. They'd found one lodged in a tree. Blood oozed from her head, a wound over her right ear, and another had clotted blood over most of her body.

"That place out there is a total disaster," one medic said. "The bad part is, it's sleeting like the devil and we can't find three people."

"How many casualties? Can you tell?" Dr. Pipkins asked, as he sent a patient to X-ray.

"Can't tell. It's like hell on earth. They're strewn all over the place."

For the next few hours, eyes and hands worked frantically to adjust IV tubes, suture lacerations, take vital signs, type blood, and start transfusions, sometimes yelling obscenities out of a frenzied effort to save life. As the evening wore on, the room became a blur of wounded; a list of anonymous victims who just happened to be at the wrong place at the wrong time.

* * *   * * *   * * *

By morning, Mercer Airlines had faxed a seating list, but as to identification it was still a hotchpotch of names that didn't necessarily match faces. The explosion had destroyed IDs and belongings that made forensic testing the only method of knowing who was who. Dental records and blood tests would come later, all of which would take time.

"Catch some shut-eye," Dr. Spraggins advised as he watched Retta wash her hands to go. Her shift had ended. "Forget about this place for a while."

"Forget?" Retta grimaced. "How can I? I've never seen anything like it."

"Need something to make you sleep?"

"No. I'm too tired to toss. Think I'll drift off the minute I hit the bed. Oh, by the way, did the older woman make it through the night?"

"Nope, sadly she didn't make it beyond the trauma center."

"Guess some poor little kids will be without a granny for Christmas."

"Probably." He shook his head. "This brush with hell hasn't been easy for any of us."

Retta didn't comment, just got her coat and headed toward the door. Too much, too quickly. She raked her dark hair back and readjusted the clasp that held it. At the door, she gasped; the streets were glazed with ice. Accidents probably at every corner and trees crackling like horsewhips. "One big mess," she yelled back.

"Drive carefully, now. Use second gear to slow and go easy on the brake," the doctor advised as she left.

Through the five blocks to her condo was another mental obstacle. She arrived home safely and unlocked the door. Fluffy, the cat, met her with a soft purr, which strangely helped to soothe her anxieties… that and a good soak in the hot tub! She'd light a candle, too, for all the casualties—poor people, and those hanging on to life by a thread. For a moment she again wondered if nursing was for her. How did one comfort a crying child? Or bring back a grandmother to her grandkids? And the poor man who kept asking for his loved ones? Christmas didn't hold much promise of joy and fun—certainly not with all the suffering.

Back at work by three the next afternoon, the accident was still all the buzz. How many and who had made it through the night? Where were their families? Had they been notified? Had data come down from Pittsburgh as to their identification, and what were the prognoses? Pat Shelby, the nurse whom Retta was to relieve, didn't say, but she did offer one bit of news—the fortyish man seemed to have stabilized. "He'll pull through, we think, but he's heavily sedated. The doctor has replaced morphine with Demerol if that means anything."

"Who is he, Pat? Have you learned?" Retta asked.

"Not sure. He continues to call for someone named *Claire* and *Persia*."

"Is he from the Middle East? He does have that dark complexion."

"Could be. Handsome guy, I'd say. And Persia? I've never heard that name for a woman, have you?"

"It might not be a woman."

"Reckon he's from Iran?" Retta continued. "I thought they all had moustaches…" Retta giggled.

"Me, too. I reckon their IDs will go to admissions first, don't you think?" Pat said more serious-like.

"Guess so." Retta got her stethoscope and glanced over the charts. "How's the young man who lost a leg?"

"Alert and talking this morning. His name is Rodney Whitworth from Houston."

"Great. Glad somebody made it."

"He's a sprinter and you know what that means. A one-legged runner." Pat shrugged. "Poor guy."

"But there are prostheses. I've seen runners use them quite well," Retta replied.

"Guess so. I'm going home. Gotta get away from this for a while," Pat said and shook her head. "I've had it."

"You and me."

Little had been said regarding the three teenage girls, well, except Dr. Copeland had mentioned that the one with all the chestnut hair had a punctured skull, which meant she might have memory loss… at least temporarily. A shame, too; she was so young, Retta thought, almost in tears. "I wonder who she is."

By noon the ICU was a conglomerate of tubes, monitors, and machines that clicked and hummed as they measured and processed bodily functions. Retta eased in and took a peek just as one of the patients began to flail her arms. Retta tiptoed over and asked, "How do you feel?"

The young woman opened her eyes. "My muscles ache. Could I have a pain pill?"

"I'll see. What has your doctor said?" Retta saw no instructions for medications.

"I feel like I might need to vomit," the young woman mumbled.

Retta looked around to see the ICU nurse enter. "She says she's about to vomit. Do you have something for her? This isn't my ward."

"I have it here. How's your leg, Candace?" the ICU nurse asked. "Her name is Candace Goodman. She's from Dallas."

"I won't make it home for Christmas, I know." Her eyes misted and her brow furrowed.

"You don't know. You might."

"At least I made it through the crash. I'm alive."

"Sure did, hon. Here's your medication."

Retta stepped back as not to interfere.

"Who is this one?" Retta asked after Candace closed her eyes.

"That's Persia Plemons. Doesn't she have the cutest nose, and look at those lips. But *Persia*? I've wondered about her. That fortyish man was calling her name over and over. Are they related?"

"Gosh, I don't know. I guess so if he was calling her name. Unusual name, I'd say. I mean, other than the ancient country," the ICU nurse said and appeared puzzled.

"They could very well be from the Middle East, but what are they doing in Oklahoma City?" Retta mumbled and raised an eyebrow. "You don't reckon they're spies?" she whispered.

"That's all we need. A plane crash, an ice storm, and an invasion of spies," the ICU nurse squeaked in a frivolous fashion.

"Crazy."

"We do have to mix a little fun in from time to time."

"Absolutely," Retta blurted with a giddy expression.

CHAPTER 2

A CLOUD OF GLOOM hovered over the city for an entire week. All the destruction and grief for the dead and wounded made the disaster seem all the more serious. By Monday of the following week, streets were clear and neighborhoods affected by the ice storm had begun to rake and pile debris from areas that formerly resembled a war zone.

At the hospital, the staff had returned to their usual routines—midmorning coffee break and silly, trite jokes in the corridors.

"Got a minute?" Pat Shelby said when Retta arrived at three that afternoon.

"If you make it short."

"I got the scoop on our Mid-Easterner," she said with widened eyes and a grin. "He's gone."

"To where?"

"A chartered jet flew in from Pittsburgh to pick him up." She put the chart that she held on the desk. "And listen to this. He's not from the Middle East at all. Honey, he's an oil tycoon... owns Wesco Oil

Company down at Anadarko. His name is B. W. Plemons. Ever hear of him?"

"At Anadarko? I thought the name rang a bell. I've known of Wesco all my life," Retta replied, surprised.

"His administrative assistant came up this weekend to visit him and, I guess, to talk business."

"As a matter of fact, my dad helped build those buildings down there," Retta said. "I guess someone broke the news to him that his wife died in the crash."

"Surely. I don't know."

"The poor man's holiday is for sure ruined."

"Yeah, I think he and his wife were en route down to award Christmas bonuses," Pat added. The wife's name was *Claire*. Remember, he called for her several times."

Retta thought for a minute. "Say, is the girl up there, the one with the head injury, is she their daughter? Her name is Plemons, too."

"Don't ask me. Must be. The name isn't that common. I guess so."

"And to think we thought she might be from Iran... a spy, for Heaven's sake. Way off base! We wouldn't make good detectives." Retta giggled. "And I don't know why I didn't remember Wesco Oil. A lot of people from the Lawton area work at Wesco."

"Well, we had no way of knowing," Pat said.

"I've never met the man. He's one of the rich ones, honey, outta my class."

"Some have and some don't," Pat grinned matter-of-factly.

"But tell me, how'd he get well so fast?" Retta asked. "He had spinal injuries, didn't he?"

"And a crushed vertebra. They took him out on a gurney to fly him home, I reckon."

"Guess money can do anything, except bring back life." Retta grimaced. "Can't bring back his wife, and it's questionable that the daughter—if she is his daughter—will pull through."

"Dr. Brody is her doctor. Taking mighty good care of her, too."

"Wouldn't you know it. Some people have all the luck," Retta wailed with her hands on her hips.

"Retta," Pat snapped. "Luck? That girl may die. She's in a coma. How can you be so flippant?"

"Oh, Pat, you know what I meant. When she opens her eyes and sees him, she'll leap clear off that bed! He's Heaven-sent, gal. Half the nurses in this hospital have a crush on him."

"And you?"

"Let's not get personal, now."

"Listen, girl, you have your fantasies. I'm going home. My day is over and, look, behave yourself. Hear?"

* * *   * * *   * * *

After a quick dinner in the hospital cafeteria, Retta slipped around through the north corridor and up to ICU. Curious as to the Plemons girl, she was surprised to see that only three of the crash survivors were still confined. The Plemons girl, as Pat had said, was in a coma. The young woman from Dallas had been discharged when her parents drove up for her, and B. W. Plemons had left. The other two, still bruised and pale, lay either asleep or unconscious. Without a briefing, it was hard to say. Retta stepped up to Persia's bed and studied her face. Was she really the daughter of B. W. and Claire Plemons? There was definitely something intriguing about her; an ashen face, eyes framed by thick lashes, but red with pockets of puffy, swollen splotches about them. "Persia," Retta whispered, and touched her hand. The young woman made no response. Retta turned to go as she remembered Dr. Brody had induced the coma and it was best to let it be.

"Muns—, Muns—," Persia suddenly mumbled just as Retta reached the door. Comatose patients sometimes mumbled, she remembered from her training, and turned again to go.

"Munsy, Muns, Mum," the girl muttered, but gave no indication that she knew what she was saying.

Weird, Retta thought, and stepped back to her bed. But again, no response. Retta didn't linger, but slipped away to return to the ER. Two school kids had wrecked a motorcycle, and one was bleeding profusely. Within seconds, she was too busy to concentrate on anything else.

"The Plemons girl mumbles a lot," she said to the other nurse after she'd attended to the teens. "Is that normal for a comatose patient?"

"Oh, yeah, sometimes they do or call names. What was she saying? Could you tell?"

"Something like *mumsy*, whatever that is."

"Reckon she meant *mother*? Dr. Brody's afraid she'll have a lapse of memory," Amber Warren, the nurse next to her said.

"Really? Will it last?"

"Sure a shame, too. He's hoping it'll be temporary."

* * *   * * *   * * *

The next morning when Pat Shelby came in to relieve Retta, they had their usual morning chat. Retta brought her up-to-date on the different cases. The young man who lost a leg was to be fitted for a prosthetic leg, and there'd been no change in the two survivors still in ICU. Persia Plemons was still in a coma.

"Did her brain swell?" Pat asked.

"He's trying to prevent that," Retta signed. "It's sad."

"Poor girl."

"I know. Can you imagine what it'd be like to forget your past?"

"And she has her whole life ahead of her."

"She must be B. W.'s daughter, or could she be his wife?"

"I wouldn't think so. He's more than twice her age, "Pat said. "Guess we're not to get too inquisitive regarding our patients."

"Yep, remember what they told us in school—Don't judge your patients, just treat them," Retta added and rolled her eyes. "Look, I'm leaving," she added, heading to wash her hands. "You have a great day, and good luck, now, with the detective work." She giggled.

* * * * * * * * * *

"Good morning, Miss Plemons," Dr. Brody greeted when he entered her hospital room a week later. Time had passed; the puncture wound to her head appeared almost healed; much of the swelling had gone.

Persia turned to face him with a perplexed stare.

"Are you comfortable? Does your head ache?" he asked when she didn't respond.

"Where am I?" she mumbled a few minutes later.

"You're in the hospital in Oklahoma City. I'm Dr. Brody."

"In Pittsburgh?"

"No. You were in a plane crash here in Oklahoma. It happened during an ice storm."

"When?"

"Last week. But you're doing fine. Ready to take on a new year… 1982 with gusto." He felt her pulse.

"New year?" Persia stared with a blank stare. Her blue eyes sought his.

"In time you'll be like new." He pulled up a chair and sat facing her. "But first tell me what you remember about your past? Does grade school ring a bell? What can you recall about your teachers?" He waited for an answer.

She rubbed her fingers across her furrowed brow.

"Do you have brothers and sisters?"

Persia closed her eyes and turned away.

Dr. Brody stepped to the head of her bed to take a second look at the wound. "It's doing fine. Real good," he whispered and quietly left the room.

At the nurses' station in the ER, Retta Roark stood reviewing a patient's chart when the doctor approached. "Miss Plemons, how is she doing?" she asked the doctor.

"Making progress… well, physically. It'll take a while. Right now she's still in a fog." He continued to study her chart. "Disoriented."

"Did we ever establish her identity?" Retta asked, concerned.

"I was told that she's B. W. Plemons's daughter. That was the last report. He turned to go.

* * * *　* * * *　* * * *

Two days passed before Persia was able to sit up on the edge of the bed, which surprised her doctor when he entered the room the next morning.

"Well, how are you, Miss Plemons?" He felt for her pulse. "Have you walked yet?"

"Not yet," Persia whispered awkwardly.

"Your head ache?" Again, he stepped up to look at the wound.

"Little."

He pulled up a chair as before. "Could we visit for a few minutes this morning?"

She smiled when their eyes met.

"Can you tell me who your mother is?"

"Mumsy," she answered.

"Who?" He appeared puzzled. "Where does Mumsy live?"

She shook her head.

The questioning continued for several minutes. Finally, the doctor said, "Miss Plemons, I'm afraid you're experiencing a lapse of memory. I hope it's temporary. Sometimes, these cases don't last long; others linger for a while. Let's have you come back in six months for reevaluation. Okay?" He patted her hand in a professional manner and left the room.

* * * *   * * * *   * * * *

"Persia, this is Maud," a voice said over the telephone that afternoon. "We're at the airport. I've come to take you home to Pittsburgh. We're in a company jet. The doctors say you are to be discharged."

Persia sat stunned. "Pittsburgh?" she answered. Maud? Who was Maud?

"Yes, you're going home."

"Is Bebe going?" she said, referring to B. W., whom she'd never called *dad*. And Mumsy? Will I see her?" Thoughts were coming clearer.

"B. W.'s in Florida. Palm Beach. He needed to get away for a while."

"Palm Beach?"

"You've been there. The winter place."

"Mumsy? Where's she?"

"They didn't tell you, child?"

"Tell me what?"

"She died in the plane crash. You and your dad were just lucky, I guess."

"She died? Mumsy died?" Persia's voice cracked. "Does Bebe know?"

"He knows. I think that was the reason he wants to get away." Maud hesitated. "Look, I'm on my way to get you."

Persia laid down the phone. Maud... was she the housekeeper? Mumsy gone? Why am I going to Pittsburgh? Why did Bebe go to Florida? She staggered to stand and slowly began to dress. *Yes,* she remembered, *Maud was the housekeeper.*

CHAPTER 3

Persia recognized Maud when she came for her; the loyal housekeeper who had been with the family for years, and as far as the trip to Pittsburgh went; tiring to say the least. Persia laid her head back and closed her eyes. Too much had happened too fast!

At Clairmont, her home in Pittsburgh, Maud helped her inside and upstairs to her room. Everything about the place seemed familiar—not that she expected anything different. Dr. Brody had reminded her that she'd experience no problems with more recent events; only early childhood memories might require some time. How, she wondered, could she collect her early knowledge enough to graduate from high school, which was only months away? She'd not think about it now, she told herself. Only one thing at a time. It was great just to get home. Clairmont was Mumsy's house, Persia called it, and rightly so. Claire Plemons's print was on everything about the place.

The house, located in one of Pittsburgh's poshest neighborhoods, was more than a mere estate. It was a personally designed place, which Claire Plemons had arranged in every detail… perfection personified! An Italian villa by design, it had the features of opulence that only big money could buy. Its fourteen bedrooms, each with bath and walk-in closet, two kitchens with an elegant dining room between, a large library stocked with tomes of science, philosophy, and literature, not to mention an entertainment area spacious enough to accommodate several hundred at any time. Together, she and B. W. had traveled extensively to collect fixtures and furnishings for a house that reflected their lifestyle. As B. W. often put it, "Anything to make Claire happy." Whether it was devotion or appeasement, her request was his command.

But Claire Ceeley Plemons hadn't gone into her marriage to B. W. empty-handed. As the only child of Tom and Sarah Ceeley of upper state New York, she was accustomed to money; had wanted for nothing. The Ceeleys had money—old money that dated all the way back to the early thirties when Tom took out a loan for his first wagers in the coal and oil business. As time passed and the Great Depression ended, the couple who had saved feverishly had accumulated giant holdings in oil during its first boom, first in Pennsylvania, then in Oklahoma and Texas. Oil was on everyone's mind; wildcatters hustled to locate leases on any acreage available. Fortunes were made overnight. Tom, well known for his prospecting expertise had even gone to Saudi Arabia one year to preside over a drilling venture, which afforded Claire the opportunity to take one semester of high school in that country, where she literally fell in love with all things Middle Eastern. The tall, stylish blonde came home overwhelmed by her experience!

When Persia—a name that resulted from the visit—came on the scene, she soon detected her mother's taste for the arts; paintings and music. Claire's ability to identify works by famous artists, the Hudson River artists, French Impressionists, and early American painters, was impressive. Several originals adorned the walls at Clairmont, which Persia considered nothing short of a palace much like those she'd read about in children's books. But the large estate, as grandiose as it was, didn't always amuse her; she often felt isolated. The expensive artwork couldn't speak to her, console her, or laugh at her girlish jokes. The furnishings seemed far too formal, cold, even the sculptures in the gardens seemed nothing more than roost for pigeons. Some nights she actually felt afraid at creaks or howls of the winds. Yet, with all Claire's pampering, shopping at Bloomingdale's and Saks, she was willing to exchange the negative for the positive. Claire was a spoiled woman herself and wanted Persia to have the same advantages—even a new Porsche. Couldn't get better'n that!

"Persia," B. W. said over the phone that evening, "did you get home okay?" His voice had the usual mellowness to it.

"Yes, where are you?" Finally, there was a connection to family.

"Palm Beach. Needed to get away for a while. Guess you know about Claire." His voice cracked at the mention of his wife. "And my back still gives me fits."

"Yes, Bebe, they told me about Mumsy. I was so sorry. I cried and cried. Have you had her funeral?" For a moment Claire's image flashed before her… deep blue eyes, oval face, and flaxen hair always perfectly coiffured.

"A simple one. You know Claire was never one for sermons. It was nice and the way she'd have wanted it."

"So what exactly happened to your back?" Persia inquired.

"A ruptured disc, they said—result of the crash. Guess I can't complain, though. I did get out alive." Again, his voice cracked. "Claire didn't."

"You know, Bebe, I can't remember a thing about a crash."

"I know, baby, but in time—"

"Well, look, I'm lonesome up here in this big house. Will you be long?"

"That's why I called. You need to get back to school. It's your senior year. You must graduate from high school."

"I know, Bebe... school? But I'm so far behind. I've missed so much. All my friends..."

"I know. You think you'll do poorly and they'll laugh at you, but listen, I've arranged for a tutor to come to the house daily. You can study in the privacy of your own home, won't have to go anywhere. Besides, your principal said that you could still graduate with your class if you caught up with the requirements."

"He said that?"

"Sure did. I think you'll like this young man. His name is Anthony Elgard. He's to come tomorrow."

"That soon?"

"I think he's the one for the job; he's well educated, speaks three languages, and has a master's degree in education."

Bebe seemed mighty persistent. But, he did have a point. Bebe was smart himself and a patient man. "Okay," she finally muttered.

"Did I tell you his name? Mr. Elgard and, honey, please address him as such."

"Bebe," she snapped. I know how to be polite, use manners. I'll be nice, well, unless he's a snooty old fox." Suddenly she felt herself again; the same devilish mood.

"He's not old, twenty-four to be exact, and comes highly recommended."

"We'll see."

"You study hard and have some good grades to show me, and listen, sweetie, don't fret about the memory thing. Mr. Elgard will understand."

"Don't be long, Bebe. I miss you."

"Me, too," he said. "Miss you a lot."

* * * * * * * * * *

Persia secretly cringed with disdain when she first set eyes on her tutor the next morning. Mr. Elgard was nothing like she expected. His lanky frame, horn-rimmed glasses, and awkward demeanor was anything but hip; a geek if ever she'd seen one. Maud had directed him to the family room where he introduced himself while Persia wondered what he was up to. For a moment, she also wondered whether she'd be able to concentrate on her work in the presence of such a gauche character.

"You have a very unusual name," he said almost in a whisper. "Quite pretty." He opened his briefcase and began to arrange his papers.

"Thanks," she mumbled, uninterested in his comment.

"A family name, I guess."

"Have no idea."

"So what are your interests... music, books, sports?" he asked, changing the subject.

"All of it, I guess." She cringed. "Animals, too. I love animals."

"And math?" he asked.

"Hate it. Don't tell me I have to study it again."

"As a senior, you should have already finished your math requirements... that is, unless you want to study calculus." He looked over his glasses now lower on his nose.

"No way. Books, maybe."

"I thought we'd start with Nathaniel Hawthorn's *Scarlet Letter*. Ever read it?"

"Is that the one where the heroine had to wear a huge A on her breasts?"

"Yes." He grinned, and appeared embarrassed at her choice of words.

"I remember something about it."

For several minutes, Mr. Elgard discussed other aspects of her studies, giving her an overview of work to come, of course in consideration of her condition. Dr. Brody had sent a list of exercises to improve her memory skills.

She sat listening and occasionally yawned as he spoke. Sometimes she stared into space, or at his thin hair that was always parted in the middle. He did seem intelligent, she decided, and as the morning passed, he didn't seem quite as awkward as she first thought.

Mr. Elgard left at noon as planned with the understanding that he'd arrive the next morning at eight-thirty rather than eight. Eight was just too early; she often stayed up until midnight or beyond and awoke later in the morning. With Claire gone, Maud didn't pay much attention to the teen's schedule, as though it would have mattered anyway, and Persia was determined to report to nobody... well, she probably would have to manage Mr. Elgard some way; Bebe might check. Mr. Elgard was strict, too; she could tell already. He'd expect nice work. At least

Mumsy wouldn't be around to enforce her grip—piano lessons, ballet, and tea at Miss Trevor's twice per week. Good gosh, all that stuff seemed so passé. No fun about any of it!

Upstairs, Persia leaned back in a chair and sighed, then rubbed her palm across her brow. She'd miss Mumsy, though. Miss her a lot. She stepped to the window and looked beyond. The gardens, still cold and dormant, were in some ways similar to her own feelings… numb and confused; at times exhilarated, at other times insecure and afraid. The journey to this point of her life had been strangely happy at times, sometimes grueling. Just how it'd go from then on, she had no idea.

CHAPTER 4

ALREADY DARKNESS HAD FALLEN over Vancouver. A cold, whistling wind blew through cracks in the old warehouse walls. Sharper and colder it was; colder than anything he'd ever felt in Oklahoma. "Jessie's probably out there somewhere—Heaven knows where. Mama, too, if she's not dead from all her loose living," he thought, "and here I am—homeless at fourteen. Some life for a teen." His small body shivered beneath his jacket, the only item of cover he had. Somehow, his earlier years always flicked back to haunt him. It was the same scene he'd relived a thousand or more times: scenes of earlier days back in Oklahoma.

"Come on, Joe Dee, and eat your oatmeal. I told you not to open her door." It was his eight-year-old sister Jessie's usual gripe.

"But I want to see Mama." The five-year-old puckered to cry.

"You know we're not to go in there when a man's with her. She'll yell at us."

"Ain't no man in there."

"You don't know. Most times when she gets up late that's the reason."
Jessie buttoned her blouse and gathered her books.

"You know everything, don't cha."

"Know more'n you, and don't you go roaming about this trailer
court today while I'm at school." She frowned.

"Can't I go, too?"

"You're not old enough. Come on, eat. The school bus will be by
any minute now."

"Don't leave me." He grabbed his sister's hand.

"Mama'll wake up after a while."

"And git ready to leave again."

"I want to pass second grade, Joe Dee. I've already failed one grade."
Little brothers, what a drag! Wish Mama would wake up and tend to
'im. I wanna learn something, the young girl thought as she opened the
door to go to the bus stop. A car suddenly pulled into the driveway and
stopped. A tall, slender woman with a briefcase got out.

"Joe Dee, git on your shoes. Somebody's coming. It's a woman."

"Bringin' us something?"

"I don't know. Never saw her before."

"Hon," the stranger said, "is your mother home?"

"She's asleep—well, I guess she's asleep. We're not to disturb her.
She works late, somewhere over in Lawton."

The visitor entered. "It's important that I see her. Which room is
hers?"

Jessie stared at the woman. "The third door there, but—"

"Does your brother have shoes? It's twenty-five degrees outside.
Where are they?"

"Over there under that chair. My name's Jessie. He's Joe Dee. Mama's name is Rebecca, but everybody calls her *Becky*. My daddy died."

The woman quickly found the boy's shoes and put them on him. "I must tell your mother that I've come to take you two with me. I'm from the Child Protective Services."

"Mrs. Hartsong," the woman said when the girl directed her to her mother's bedroom. "I'm Treva Dyer."

"Who?"

"From DHS. I've come to take your children."

"Mama," the little girl pleaded, "she made me open your door. Please don't yell and please don't let her take us away."

Rebecca Hartsong, her auburn hair tousled, thick, day-old make-up smudged and caked, mumbled, "Take my children?" She roused in bed to support herself while speaking. "You can't take my children."

"I'm sorry, ma'am, but we've had numerous reports of neglect and abuse."

"Mama don't hit us," Jessie interrupted. "Well, except when we disturb her."

"Where are their clothes?" the woman asked.

Rebecca sat up momentarily. "When will I get them back?"

"That's up to you. We'll see."

A few minutes later, Jessie and Joe Dee followed the woman to her car and got in. "I don't want to go," the boy sobbed. "I want Mama."

"I can't miss another day of school, ma'am. Miss Patterson'll mark me absent," Jessie pleaded.

"I'm sorry, children, but it's my duty to find a good home for you—a home where you'll be taken care of and loved," the woman consoled as she started the car to drive away.

In the back seat, Joe Dee quietly sobbed as he clutched his sister's hand. Jessie turned to watch through the rearview window as their trailer home gradually disappeared from sight. "Don't cry, Joe Dee," she whispered to her brother. "Let's be nice—say *please* and *thank you* and maybe the lady'll bring us back home." The small boy wiped his face of tears and rested his head against his sister's shoulder.

"That was a long time ago," Joe Dee mumbled. "Here I am in Vancouver living on the street." He wiped a tear from his young face.

"For gosh sakes, boy, quit your mumbling. Ain't no way a man can sleep," the transient next to him griped. Carlos, he called himself; whether that was his real name was anybody's guess.

"Quit callin' me *boy*. My name's Joe Dee Hartsong." Hungry and depressed, he hopped up, zipped up his jacket, and dashed down the creaking attic steps. Carpy's Restaurant threw out their food scraps about ten; then later they'd dump their dinner leftovers. After two months on the street, he'd figured it out; get there early before others came out of hiding. Darkness brought out the homeless, like termites on their spring flight, to dig into garbage cans, dumpsters, or food anywhere they found it. Crazy way to live, he told himself, but it worked—well, most of the time.

Downstairs, a whiff of December air smacked him in the face, but too distraught and hungry to turn back, he bristled and hurried to the back alley behind Carpy's. More than once, he'd dug for warm fries, onion rings, even portions of uneaten burgers... nothing short of a perfect meal for a teen!

The alley was dark, almost eerie. Only a few rays from a street light detailed the heavy metal container. Quietly, he sneaked up and was about to jump up on the rim to balance his boyish frame when a tall, lean figure emerged from behind a wall. Joe Dee jumped, startled. Of all the times he'd come, he'd seen no one—not even restaurant employees. He leaned against a wall and waited as his belly rumbled from hunger and his blond, shaggy hair blew about his brow.

"Whatcha doin', boy?" a deep voice blurted, and the tall man stepped forward.

"What's it to you?" Joe Dee sassed, too hungry for interruption.

"Go home and let yo mama feed ya."

"Ain't got no mama," Joe Dee said and bent into the dumpster. One fact he'd learned from street life was to ignore bullies. Most of them were full of bluff, anyway.

"Did you hear what I said?" the stranger scoffed and gave him a ghastly glare, then suddenly with a yank of his jacket collar tossed the boy a good five feet. "That'll teach ya. Scram!"

Joe Dee sulked away, hungry. He'd return later for another try.

CHAPTER 5

At a street corner not far away, he saw a group of young people assembled, singing and laughing. Two musicians soon broke into a tune that sent the crowd into a joyful commotion. Feeling shy and self-conscious, he edged up behind the crowd to join, and for a moment no one seemed to notice, but when a young girl stepped up, he cringed. She was pretty, well, considering her obviously dyed hair as black as a crow. Her eyes were clear blue and didn't match at all with her lips and nails painted as purple as a baby's cold bottom.

"You lost?" she asked as if she'd noticed his uneasiness.

"Nawh, why?"

"Where you from?" she asked. Her eyes danced as she spoke.

"Portland." He hesitated. "Well, Oklahoma, really—Duncan, Oklahoma or Carlisle, I guess I oughta say."

"Where?"

"Carlisle. Near Lawton."

"You run away?"

"Yep."

"Why? Your dad hard on ya?"

"Nawh, just cause." He hesitated again. "Ain't got no dad."

"Look, I'm Addie." She smiled sweetly.

He moved about nervously until he spotted a patrol car coming, then darted toward the back of the crowd. It was the way he'd learned to evade the law; at fourteen he was supposed to still be in school.

The girl followed him. "Wanna cigarette?" she asked. "Here, sit by me."

"Sure," Joe Dee said, reaching for it as he suddenly remembered something his mother once said. "Son, don't ever start to smoke. It's a dirty, filthy habit." He ignored it and lit up. What right did she have to advise him after all her boozing?

"You're cute," Addie said staring into his large amber eyes. "You got dimples."

It was the first compliment he'd had in ages. What was a guy supposed to say? "Thanks," he mumbled self-consciously.

"Like Vancouver?" Addie asked as they moved to the curb.

"Yeah, sure. Nice. Where do you live?"

"On Vine Street, and you? I mean here in Vancouver."

He hesitated. Did he have to divulge the fact that he slept in an abandoned warehouse—with a dozen or more other transients? "Uh, on the other side of town," he said knowing he'd lied. "Long way from here."

"You can go home with me," she said and smiled again.

Joe Dee froze. Did the girl mean that he could sleep with her? He'd never slept with a girl. Guess there was a first time for everything. He didn't answer but glanced at a clock across the street—ten to twelve. The dumpster! Without comment, he got up and turned to go.

"Where you going?" Addie asked.

"I promised a friend I'd meet him," Joe Dee muttered.

"Will you come back?"

"Probably."

"I'll look for you." She gazed into his eyes as though sad to see him go. "I thought you were coming home with me."

"Might later," he responded and walked away.

This time the dumpster was clear, deserted. Joe Dee jumped up on the rim to balance himself in order to reach the contents. Pulling out several pieces of food still warm, he stuffed his empty stomach until it wouldn't take more.

The crowd had scattered by the time he returned. Whatever Addie had had in mind for the night was now cancelled. She was nowhere to be seen. A light snow began to spit; time to go in, he told himself as he meandered toward the warehouse.

By the time he reached the attic, Carlos was sitting against the wall puffing on a cigarette butt. A heap of at least two dozen lay beside him. He'd picked them up off the street and brought them up to finish off. "Where you been, boy?" he blurted and took another drag.

"I told you not to call me *boy*. My name is Joe Dee Hartsong. I met a girl tonight," Joe Dee said, deciding to ignore Carlos's comments. "She asked me to go home with her." He sat down beside Carlos.

"You didn't? What kind of fool is that? Boy, I mean Joe Dee, you gotta learn better'n that."

"I went to eat and when I got back she had gone. Pretty, too, and friendly."

"Gone, aye? Next time you won't leave, I guess." Carlos snuffed out another cigarette butt and smoothed his scruffy beard. His face was weathered and his small, beady eyes showed redness. By his own account, he'd spent fifteen years on the street.

"She probably thought I smelled bad. Is there anywhere around here a man can shower?"

"Some gym, probably, if you'd agree to take out the garbage or sweep the floor. And where can a guy get a blanket? It's damn cold up here."

"A church, I guess. They sometimes hand them out. Here," Carlos said, "take this." He handed him a soiled, tattered one. "But look, boy, you need to go home to your family… school. This street life ain't no way to live."

"Butt out, Carlos. I told you I don't have a family." Joe Dee smirked. Why wouldn't Carlos mind his own business?

"No brothers or sisters?"

"A sister." Joe Dee grimaced. "Her name is Jessica, but I call her Jessie… have no idea where she is, though. Could be dead for all I know."

"Dead?" Carlos inquired, growing more personal in his questioning.

"Look, man, I don't ask you crazy questions. Lay off. Said I don't know and that's it." Joe Dee got quiet and lay back on the blanket that Carlos had given him. Any mention of life back in Oklahoma always depressed him.

Carlos stared at him.

"Guess you think I'm too young to be on the streets," Joe Dee said and closed his eyes.

31

Carlos finished the cigarette butt on his lip and settled in himself.

* * * * * * * * * * * *

The next morning, Joe Dee didn't dwell too long on the beauty of the landscape when he saw that a thick snow had fallen… it was time for breakfast!

Snow on sidewalks and parks, places where he often picked up loose coins for donuts and coffee, had made breakfast next to impossible. And if some charity was to hand out food, he had heard nothing of it. Hunger pangs that began under his rib cage and extended downward was reason enough to leave the warehouse early for the morning search. Careful not to wake Carlos or any of the dozen or more others sprawled on the floor, he zipped his jacket and eased down the stairs.

Turning up his collar against the wind, he lowered his hands in his pockets as far as they'd go and set out for the corner of Ash and Elmwood where he'd met Addie the night before. She wouldn't be there, but he couldn't resist the urge to check. Carlos was right; he'd acted a fool by not taking her up on her offer. She'd reached out to him, smiled, and accepted him. Why he'd walk away, he had no idea.

At the corner, as expected, the crowd had gone. Addie, like others in his life, had disappeared like a vapor over a pond. Sadly, he turned to go and headed toward Carpy's. Ordinarily, he waited until dark to visit the dumpster, but hunger urged him on; he seldom missed breakfast. It was the only motivation to face a new day.

At the dumpster, though, he met disappointment again… the darn lid was down, closed. Snow lay thick on it making it much too heavy to lift. Disgusted, he stared at it, then left.

"Carlos," he said back at the warehouse—Carlos was awake and sat puffing on another cigarette butt. "Never been so hungry in my life. Everything's covered with snow."

"What day is this?" Carlos thought for a minute. "Friday, it is. Pastor Raymie's church usually offers a hot meal on Fridays. Wanna go?"

"One of them preachers, huh? Always talking about sin. In no mood for that."

"Never heard 'im say nothing about it. Their hot vegetables and gravy shore fills a fella up. Come go with me."

Joe Dee, half persuaded, remembered that Pastor Raymie might notice his small size, youth, and report him to Family Services or the police. No way he'd get into that. Not that them folks didn't mean well. There had to be more excitement out there somewhere that he'd not discovered yet. No, the trip to Pastor's church was out. Carlos didn't pursue it, merely appeared surprised, especially on such a cold winter day. He'd learned already that the boy had a determined streak. He'd find food on his own.

Joe Dee, bored and hungry, curled up on the tattered blanket and pretended to go to sleep while Carlos, quiet now, puffed on a cigarette butt. It was around ten when Carlos readied to leave for the church. Again, he straightened his beard and smoothed his hair for the trip for lunch.

By noon, Joe Dee decided to return to the dumpster in the hope that sunlight had melted the snow on the heavy lid. Zipping his jacket, he set out. On the street below, he asked a woman for a few coins, but she smirked and walked on.

At the dumpster, his luck was no better. The snow had gone, but the lid was still down and too heavy for him to lift. Vancouver was cold, too cold and hard for someone in his shoes, no funds and only the clothes on his back. He needed to head south, not to Duncan or Carlisle, but somewhere warmer, perhaps California.

Back at the warehouse, he again lay back on the blanket and thought. In L.A. he might get a job as a groom at the horse stable on a movie set. Why hadn't he thought of it sooner? Be warmer there, too. Without debate, his decision gelled. Yep, he'd get up early the next morning, walk the ten or twelve blocks out to the main thoroughfare, and head south. Yeah, hitch a ride south! Something in his boyish head seemed to have clicked, especially when he thought of horses... the only aspect of life that he really enjoyed.

Suddenly, memories of the Murphy's in Duncan surfaced, especially Rusty, his horse. Me and him were a pair... good team. Each day when I came home from school, there he'd be standing beside the gate waitin'. Joe Dee felt tears swell and jumped up to run down the stairs... get out of the attic that allowed too much time for reflection. "There's gotta be a better place than this," he complained, ready to set his idea into action.

Chapter 6

Awake earlier than usual, Joe Dee sat up and glanced toward Carlos, still deep in sleep. A trickle of urine oozed down the man's leg; he'd wet his pants again and reeked of it. Best not to wake him to say goodbye. What was the point? He stood, straightened his jacket, and descended the rickety stairs to the outside, happy to leave the dusty old attic.

Outside, most of the snow had melted and overhead patches of sun shone through breaks in the clouds. Facing a cold wind, he set out toward the outskirts of the city where an interchange of highways led in various directions. If luck smiled on him, someone headed south might give him a lift, might take him all the way into L.A., and with his knowledge of horses, employment as a groom for a movie company could become a reality. He could only hope; he needed the money. His jeans were slick with grime and his sneakers full of holes.

At a sign that read *Seattle*, he stopped and cocked his thumb with a grin as wide as the Mississippi just as a semitrailer approached but soon zoomed past. Disappointed, he stepped back. With any luck at all, he could be in Seattle within a couple of hours and on to L.A. within a couple of days. Thoughts of warm sunny weather, certainly less snow, stirred his passions—another rig whizzed toward him and like the previous one soon disappeared down the highway. Traffic was heavy. Saturday morning meant travelers were on the go. When another semi approached, he again stepped up and cocked his thumb. Luckily, the darn thing stopped! Totally awed by the size of the rig, he jumped up to catch the door latch and to see a ruddy-faced driver make a thumbs-up sign.

"Going south?" Joe Dee asked, too excited to question the integrity of the driver. A ride was a ride.

"L.A. or in that direction. Get in. Where you headed?" The man's voice was kind enough, but concern showed on his fiftyish face. "You look kinda young, son. How old are you?"

Joe Dee adjusted himself in the deep leather seat that felt like Heaven to his cold rear. "Fourteen. Be fifteen in February."

"Thought you might be twelve."

Joe Dee grinned. "Sure appreciate the lift. You go all the way into L.A.?"

"Anaheim. It's in the Los Angeles area. I haul produce for some grocers in the area. Two loads per week." The driver stopped at the light. "Where you from?"

"Oklahoma, mostly." Joe Dee had already fixated on a box of donuts on the dashboard. "My name's Joe Dee Hartsong."

"Help yourself to the donuts. My name is Chuck. Aren't you young to be so far from home?"

"Guess so." Joe Dee had no intentions of getting into details. He reached for a donut, convinced that an angel of mercy had smiled on him—a ride all the way to L.A. and warm donuts! Ravished, he bit into one to taste the sweet warm treat! "Nice rig you have here," he commented as he ate. "You sleep in here?"

"Sure do. I have two beds. One behind me and one that pulls down."

"Mind if I have another donut?" Joe Dee asked, feeling more at ease.

"Sure, help yourself. Care for some coffee? It's there in the thermos." The man pointed to the area between them.

"You could almost live in this thing," Joe Dee said, observing the truck's features. "Sure a lot of knobs and buttons. You have a handle?"

"Yeah, *Bucco-locco*. Don't use it much, though... well, except when I want to talk with someone on the road. That's not too often, always in too bigga hurry."

"How'd you learn to drive this rig?"

"Mostly on my own. They gave me a week's instruction, mostly in turning. This boy's hard to turn... mighty big to get around corners."

"Ever had a wreck?"

"Nothing major. Slid off on an icy shoulder once."

Joe Dee poured himself a cup of coffee and looked about. From the truck cab the view was beautiful; evergreen trees, an occasional spit of snow, not to mention far away hills and mountains. Chuck slowed as signs of the Canadian-U.S. border came up. At a checkpoint, he showed proper identification and moved on.

"I haul mostly in the States," Chuck said. "You say you're from Oklahoma? Where in Oklahoma?"

"Down close to Lawton. Duncan was the last place," Joe Dee said reluctantly. Surely Chuck wasn't planning to question him a lot, then go and turn him in to the police. "Just lived there three years was all… a foster home, it was."

"Is Duncan close to Oklahoma City? I've been to the city," Chuck stated.

"South of it. Ever hear of the Old Chisholm Trail? Duncan's right along it." Joe Dee untied his shoe laces and slipped his cold feet out. The heat in the truck felt soothing to his toes. "Horse country, too. Oklahoma has lots of 'em. Yeah, cowboys would drive their cattle along that old trail all the way up to Abilene, Kansas, to market." A broad grin broke across his face. The thought of horses or cowboys lifted his spirits.

"You like horses, I take it."

"Yep, sure do. I even broke a wild mustang once… me and a neighbor. He gave me a few pointers, but I done most of it. Most fun I ever had."

"Where'd you get it?"

"Montana. Some folks got two, then decided they couldn't handle 'em and gave me one." Joe Dee's eyes widened as he spoke. "One pretty horse, he was. *Rusty* was his name. Sorrel with bay tail and mane; points they call 'em." To mention Rusty's name brought tears to his eyes.

"So how did you calm 'im down? Beat the stuffin' outta 'im?" The driver turned toward him with a questioning look.

"Nawh, can't whip a horse, not one you're trying to break. I never hit Rusty, ever. That's no way they'd gain your trust if you did. Mustangs have a lot of fear anyway… predators in the wild. Mountain lions mostly. They'll take a wild horse down. No, it don't help a thing to beat one."

"I saw a movie once where a trainer ran one in circles for hours. What was that for? Seemed crazy to me," Chuck said and frowned.

"Tiring 'im. When a horse gets tired, he's more willing to notice you... calm down and listen to you." Joe Dee grinned. "Betcha didn't know that wild mustangs have a lead horse, usually a mare. Sure do. Yeah, when a trainer is breaking one, the trainer becomes the lead horse. They have lots of sense, too."

"Never heard it that way."

"Yep, it's the truth. My neighbor in Oklahoma told me. Gave me lots of good tips."

"How long did it take? I mean to break 'im?"

"Bout three weeks. It was funny, though, how soon I started seeing signs that he was coming around; listening to me."

"How could you tell?"

"At first, he'd cock an ear toward me, like he was listening when I spoke to 'im or called his name. Then he'd wiggle his upper lip as a signal that he heard me. Wasn't long after that that he'd lower his head on command. I knew he was ready for the saddle."

"Sounds like you know all about horses," Chuck commented as he passed a car on the road. "Who's tending to 'im now that you're out here?"

"He's gone... yep, have no idea where he is. My dad up and sold 'im one day while I was at school. Almost killed me, too."

"Sold 'im? How come?"

"I made two F's on my report card. He said I was spending too much time with Rusty. I just up and left. Slipped out of the house that night and hitched a ride toward Montana. Ended up in Portland, though."

"Does your dad know where you are?" Chuck asked curiously.

"No, that's why I move around. Didn't stay in Portland but two weeks. Went on to Vancouver. I just figured Dad couldn't love a son much if he up and sold his horse. He was my foster dad, anyway."

"Think he mighta wanted you to do well in school?"

"Can't prove it by me what he wanted. I sure as the devil won't go back. Yeah, Rusty was my pal... loved that horse. Could talk to 'im and he'd listen. Cock his ear toward me. Every day after school I rushed out to ride 'im." Joe Dee looked out toward the city of Seattle. "Nawh, I ain't ever going back to Oklahoma."

"Your real folks divorced, I guess." Chuck glanced toward the boy to see tears in his eyes.

"Dead, I reckon. My dad is dead for sure. He fell off a scaffold at his work and died. Jessie was my sister, but I don't know where she is." Joe Dee stopped talking. "That's why I loved my horse so; he was all I had."

"Well, look," Chuck said kindly. "Why don't we stop for some food?"

Joe Dee's spirits perked. Food! A real meal. "But you won't turn me in to the cops, will you, sir, I mean, Chuck? I mean for running away. I want to stay in L.A. They'll send me right back to Oklahoma."

Chuck didn't answer, just refilled his mug with coffee and turned off the engine.

CHAPTER 7

AFTER A GOOD MEAL and restroom stop, Chuck turned the big rig around and started southward. Joe Dee marveled at his ability to handle the eighteen-wheeler.

"Should be in Oregon soon," Chuck said and gave the boy a momentary glance. "You say you spent time in Portland?"

"Two weeks was all. Thought I might find work there—at a shoeshine stand or something, but nothing panned out. They'd just look at me strange-like and walk away. Met some nice kids, though. Spent most of the time down at Pioneer Square. That's where they all hang out."

"I thought it was sixteen to work publicly. That child labor law."

"Can't prove it by me. I just needed work to eat."

"So what did you do in Vancouver?"

"Bummed around mostly."

"No work there, either?" Chuck watched the highway. Traffic was heavy.

"Afraid to stir much. Fraid the cops would find me and pick me up. Everybody thinks I'm about twelve. I'm used to it, though. My sister used to call me *runt*, especially when she got mad at me."

Chuck glanced at him again with a raised eyebrow. "Yeah?"

"The cops'd send me straight to one of them shelters and from there back to Oklahoma."

"What grade did you study back in Duncan?"

"Seventh. I failed one year and guess I would've failed this'n. I don't care for school. Rather be around horses." Joe Dee tossed his hair to the side. "The kids always called me names—*weasel* and *little butt*. Embarrassing as hell."

"I'd kick some butt myself if I's you and get back in school."

Joe Dee got quiet. "Didn't stay in one place long enough to learn anything or make friends… well, except with the Murphys. I was with them three years and they acted like they wanted to adopt me, then he up and sold my horse. That ain't no way to get somebody to love ya." Joe Dee shook his head in disgust.

* * * * * * * * * *

The drive through Oregon was nice. The snow-capped Cascades seemed like a winter wonderland. The long stretch of highway lay ahead like a grosgrain ribbon.

"You got a girl?" Chuck asked, turning to Joe with a grin. "Bet Oklahoma has some pretty ones."

"Met one in Vancouver. She was cute. Her name was Addie. Even asked me to go home with her one night."

"You didn't?" Chuck laughed. "You better wise up, boy. If a gal asked me, I'd sure go."

"Guess I did act stupid. I left to go eat and when I got back, she was gone; couldn't find her anywhere. Just like my sister back in Oklahoma."

"How long ago was that?" Chuck asked. "That you last saw your sister?"

"Soon be ten years. I was five."

"That long?"

"I might not even know her if I saw her." Joe Dee looked away over the landscape. "Can't remember much about her, except how she cried when some woman came to take her. She wanted me to go, too, but they wouldn't let me. Said they might come for me later, but they never did." His eyes misted again. "Jessie was her name. She tended to me while Mama was at work, except when she had to go to school." A lump came to his throat. His voice cracked. "When everybody left, I went down to the creek to look for frogs."

"You've had a hard life, my boy," Chuck said with a sympathetic look.

"Yep, nothing much excitin' about losing a family." He got quiet again. "And to think I still have my sister's locket." Joe Dee pulled the small piece of jewelry from his flattened wallet and held it for Chuck to see. Only part of her I still have, and I wouldn't take anything for it."

"I'll be doggone. How come you have it?"

"I was always begging to wear it and had it on when the woman took her away. No time to pull it off and give it back." His eyes filled with tears. "Guess I'll never lay eyes on her again."

At the edge of the city, Chuck pressed the brake and said, "I don't go into L.A. I go around it. I guess this is as far as I can take you, son, but look—here's a ten-dollar bill to help you along." He handed it to Joe

43

Dee and lowered his glance to face the boy. "You be careful out there. The world's a mighty big place."

"Thanks," Joe Dee said. "Thanks, too, for the ride. Didn't mean to bore you with a sob story." He jumped from the cab and hurried to a nearby truck stop.

Inside, a middle-aged woman worked the counter and cash register. When Joe appeared, she turned to face him and asked what he needed.

"Can you tell me how to get to Universal Studios?"

"The Hollywood area?" The woman seemed surprised.

"Guess so. I'm not from here. I'm trying to find work."

"Work? How old are you?" she inquired with a puzzled stare.

"Fourteen, uh, almost fifteen."

"Where you from?"

"Oklahoma. Duncan, Oklahoma. I know a lot about horses, too. Thought I might find work as a groom."

When the young woman turned away, Joe Dee turned, too, to explore the other end of the building. The aroma of burgers and fries wafted through the place, and with the ten in his pocket, he soon followed the food trail; he was famished.

Seated at a table near the back door, he suddenly caught sound of a man's voice up front where he'd spoken with the woman.

"You say you got a kid in here?" the man said. "A runaway, you think?"

"Yep, I think sure it's this kid on this poster." She pointed. "Looks just like him and he said he's from Oklahoma."

Joe Dee realized what was up and jumped from the chair and out the back door. Before the officer could find him, he was far down the alley and lost into the night.

* * * *   * * * *   * * * *

Three weeks passed before Joe Dee stepped out the door of the homeless shelter where he'd slept in L.A. and felt the sole of his right sneaker flop off. His jeans showed more grime, too, that rubbed his thigh, making it difficult to walk, and his own body odor made him want to vomit. L.A. had been eye-opening to say the least, but to find work was next to impossible. If Universal Studios maintained horse stables, he couldn't find them. "Heck," he mumbled, heading east but not sure where he'd go. Out on the highway, he threw up his thumb to hitch a ride, and within minutes a Chevy pickup eased up to the curb and stopped.

"Where ya headed?" a clean-shaven man asked. "Need a ride?"

"Thought I'd look around for ranches; I need work. I'm a horse whisperer."

The stranger stared at him, obviously surprised. His brow above his gray-green eyes creased into a frown. "You are? I'd think you'd be in school."

It was the same song second verse that he'd heard so often. "I'm taking time off to find part-time work. My mom needs help with the bills." Joe Dee realized he lied, but what else could he say?

"You live in L.A.?" the driver asked.

"Yeah, uh, yes sir," Joe Dee answered. "I'm in the eighth grade, but my real goal is to race horses. I know a lot about 'em."

"Where'd you learn?"

"My uncle. He halter breaks and trains wild mustangs. He taught me."

"Around here?"

"In Montana." Again, Joe Dee knew he'd lied. "Know anybody around here who might take me on part-time?"

The man appeared to believe him. He quit his questioning and said, "Ranches? Apple Valley has ranches. Roy Rogers's ranch is out that way."

"Roy Rogers? The cowboy? The actor? You're kiddin'."

"No. You need to see it if you like horses." The driver pressed the brake. "It's northeast of here."

"You goin' that way?"

"No, I'm going south. I'll turn out here at the intersection."

At the next traffic light, the driver slowed and pulled over. "Good luck, now," he said when Joe Dee readied to get out.

"Thanks a lot. Sure do thank ye, sir."

"You be careful," the driver said and pulled away. Joe Dee didn't answer, but with his head full of fantasies jumped onto the sidewalk and into a shop to inquire as to how to reach Apple Valley.

At Lucerne Valley, a sign with an arrow pointed north—Apple Valley and Victorville. Highway 18 led to it. The area around Lucerne Valley was beautiful, flat with mountains to the side. He could almost picture himself astride a horse on a balmy California day with the wind in his face! He hurried along with nothing less than Roy Rogers's ranch in mind. Roy wouldn't be there. Seems like he'd read or heard that Roy died, he told himself, but with any luck at all he might just see Roy's horse, Trigger... or had Trigger died, too? Too much had happened for him to know such things. He stopped suddenly when he saw a sign with the name *Crosswinds Farms—Thoroughbreds and Palominos*. His heart raced! *Sally Connors*, it stated was the owner. A painting of two galloping steeds was under her name. Joe Dee stopped and stared at the sign. A long, winding driveway led down to the residence—a spacious ranch-style house. Impressed with what he saw, he ambled down the drive to inquire. Could she need a groom or stable boy?

The house was imposing... larger than anything he'd ever seen except in the movies. Eagerly, he rang the bell and waited. In a few minutes, a stout, graying woman opened the door and stared. "Yes," she scoffed.

"Ma'am, I'm Joe Dee Hartsong. I saw your sign and wondered if you might need a good stable boy or mucker?" If there was anything he didn't like, it was to muck stables, but something was better'n nothing, he told himself.

"No," she snapped and slammed the door in his face."

Devastated, he trudged back to the main road and headed on east, disappointed and hungry.

Approximately two miles beyond, he saw another sign. It was mid-afternoon; he was in no mood for another ugly encounter, but what the heck? *Whispering Trails* the sign read. Again, he hurried to the door and rang the bell.

"Ma'am," he began when a tall, trim woman appeared before him. Her silver hair, drawn back attractively, revealed a face immaculately made up and the bluest eyes he'd ever seen. "I'm looking for part-time work. I see you own horses."

"Yes, a few. What kind of work?"

"With horses—a groom probably or stable boy." Joe Dee made sure he used his best manners. "It's after three and school is out for the day. I wondered if I might work three or four hours after school each day." He realized he'd lied again, but it got easier each time. "I could muck stables or take care of the tack. I know a lot about horses."

The woman eyed him as she ran her long fingers across her brow. "I'm Claudia McClish, a widow, and yes, I do hire extra help from time to time. Tell me, where and what do you know about horses?" Her blue eyes sparkled as she spoke; she had a pleasant way about her.

"I helped my uncle train a wild mustang once. Did most of it myself and had that little colt eating right outta my hand in no time." He grinned proudly. "I know I can do it."

"You look kinda young for all that."

"But ma'am, I'm almost fifteen, well, next week as a matter of fact."

Claudia continued to eye him with a cautious expression. "You actually broke one of the wild ones?"

"Yeah, my uncle in Montana taught me. They have a world of horses out there. In fact, that's where he got his mustang."

"Well, as a matter of fact, a friend of mine has offered me one—a mustang for my daughter. Actually, she's my godchild. Roslynn is her name, and I thought it'd make a great birthday gift. She's to turn thirteen next week and has begged for a horse for a couple of years now."

"Oh, yes, ma'am." His heart leaped to his throat. Was something about to gel?

"What was your name again?" she asked.

"Joe Dee Hartsong."

"And you're in eighth grade?"

"Yes, ma'am."

"Would you care to take a look at the stables? I have two thoroughbreds and a palomino. I may have told you. The palomino is a yearling? She smiled. "He's a pretty little thing."

"Oh, yes ma'am. I could start this afternoon if you'd like. Do you want me to muck your stables?"

Claudia didn't answer, but directed him to the back, talking constantly as she went.

From that moment on, something clicked between Joe Dee and Claudia. She listened when he spoke. She smiled a lot, which gave him confidence, and she seemed eager to have his help. The idea of his experience with a wild mustang must have impressed her. Before the afternoon ended, Joe Dee felt totally at ease with her, tickled to have found a job!

"So you want me to start tomorrow afternoon?" he asked, about to leave.

"I do. I think the corral is ready and I expect the mustang in about a week. In the meantime, you can clean the stables and rearrange the tack shop."

"Sounds good." Joe Dee hesitated. "I was wondering, ma'am, if you might forward me a little money. I need some new shoes. Just a few dollars would help."

Claudia McClish glanced down toward his feet. She frowned at the sight of his shoes. "How much?" she asked and started for her purse.

"Twenty or thirty would be enough," he said enthusiastically, his heart beating much too fast.

"Joe," she said, omitting the *Dee* in his name. "Let me give you a hundred. Get yourself some new jeans and a shirt, too. Come back tomorrow afternoon and I'll put you to work." She handed him two crisp fifty-dollar bills.

"Yes ma'am, you can trust me. I'll sure be back. Sure will, ma'am."

"My goddaughter will dance all over this place when I tell her about the mustang." Claudia laughed.

"Be right here at three. You can count on me."

"Now listen, Joe. My name's *Claudia*. Drop the *ma'am* stuff. It makes me feel old. Call me *Claudia*, and I'll call you *Joe*. Okay?"

He nodded with the cash already deep in his pocket. He turned to go and was almost out the door when he heard her call. "Oh, Joe, I almost forgot. Could you bring me a permission note from your parents? You're not yet sixteen."

Shocked, he turned to stare. Had he heard her correctly. "Note?"

"Yes, I like to be on the safe side with my employees."

"Er, uh, yes'm," he stuttered, perplexed. There was no way in the world he could bring a note! He had no parents. Damn, just as I thought I had a job!

CHAPTER 8

THE STOP AT CLAUDIA McCLISH'S place had finally reaped results! She owned horses and she needed help with them… nothing short of sheer luck, he told himself. And for the life of him, he'd not blow it. If push came to shove regarding a permission note from his parents, why, he'd say he forgot it or forge the darn thing. Anything to prevent the loss of a good job. He picked up his pace toward Victorville with cash in his pocket and the thrill of getting to train another mustang in his head! It was a dream come true. Claudia McClish had money; funds so necessary in the racing business. If his work with her proved successful, she might also furnish references and connections for greater opportunities to come… whatever that might prove to be. For once in his young life, things were going his way… well, except the mustang deal *did* remind him of Rusty, his horse back in Oklahoma, and the Murphys. They *were* good folks. Too bad his stay with them suddenly ended. On the other hand, had he stayed around Duncan, he might never have found Claudia and Whispering Trails… and her beautiful thoroughbreds.

In Victorville, he entered the mega-mart and soon purchased some new duds… jeans, two t-shirts, and a pair of sneakers. Without delay, he hurried to the men's restroom, totally exuberant, to freshen up. Luckily, the place was empty, and without hesitation, he splashed warm water under his arms, over his torso, and over his head and face. A new feeling of success came over him; he had found his place in this Los Angeles suburb and nothing would pry him from it.

Finished with his freshening, he realized he had no place to sleep. Outside, he saw the sun in its plunge below the horizon. Where? He gasped; would he find lodging? Victorville was small, no place for homeless shelters or boarding houses, and a park bench in January was out of the question. Vancouver all over again, he told himself, frantic at the prospects, as he set out toward the business district—as small as it was—with the hope that something would turn up.

Nothing resulted, and by ten he, weary and stressed, got another idea… the men's restroom at the mega-mart. He'd go inside, amble around until late, then take the last stall inward, latch the door, and curl up on the floor for the night. At least it'd be safe and warm. Unless discovered and yanked out, the night would pass!

**** **** ****

The plan worked. The next morning, Joe again splashed himself and headed out for coffee and donuts. He had cash! If the morning progressed as planned, he'd arrive at the Roy Rogers Museum when it opened.

With forty-five dollars of Claudia's money still in his pocket, Joe found his way to the museum and for two hours engrossed himself in every aspect of the famous cowboy's life. The Western cowboy aura with lassos and horses was of utmost interest; the place was far more than he expected. Photos of Roy and Trigger were posted everywhere over the place, not to mention photos of Roy and Dale. All of it spurred his enthusiasm. How did one rise to such prominence, he wondered. He'd ask Claudia. His heart pounded at the thought that he'd met someone who shared his love of horses and had the funds to run such a successful operation. He also wondered how she'd come into such wealth, and to think he'd soon be a part of it. Surely, his lucky star had landed him right into Whispering Trails, and he wanted to get familiar with every aspect of it!

Whispering Trails had been a dream come true for Ted and Claudia McClish. Ted's family, wealthy from the silver mining days in New Mexico, had passed down an enormous fortune to Ted, their only son, whose life-long dream was to own and race thoroughbreds. But after his initial purchase of two, one two-year-old, which he named *High Pockets*, and a one-year-old yearling, *Blazzy Star*, he suffered a fatal heart attack. Claudia was left with everything! Undaunted by the responsibilities and expenses necessary to run such an operation, she was determined to keep the ranch and continue what she and Ted had begun. The fact that she knew horses herself helped—she knew how to hire the expertise needed to make good trades and purchases at auctions. She had connections to trainers and buyers, too, who advised her with such. And it didn't hurt that Claudia, herself, was congenial, nice, and easy to talk with; folks liked her and were willing to help her, which Joe had already noticed. He liked her, too, and was more than anxious to get back to Whispering Trails at three that afternoon.

"Hi, there," Claudia yelled when she saw him walk up. The mustang was already in the corral, rearing and huffing wildly... a pretty colt, sorrel in color, appeared at least fifteen hands in height, mighty good-looking specimen, but oh, so spirited!

"You got 'im, I see," Joe said, stepping to meet her.

"Vance Mangrum brought 'im over this morning. Said he couldn't handle 'im and wanted to know if I could take 'im early."

Joe grinned proudly. Claudia was counting on him, it was obvious. "Looks good," he replied. "Mighty good colt."

"Wild little devil," Claudia said.

Joe stepped out to the corral and opened the gate. The colt ran in the opposite direction with its head in the air and tail blowing in the wind. Joe stepped behind the colt and extended his hand. The horse ran faster. "This boy's got stamina." Joe stood staring. "He'll come around, though. It just takes time." He extended his hand again and the colt responded in the same manner. "Got a white shopping bag?"

Claudia appeared puzzled. "Bag?"

"Yeah, to put over my head. He'll stop and look... I'll get his attention."

She, neatly clad in jeans and shirt, ran to the back porch for the bag. "This okay?" she said returning.

Joe slipped it over his head and walked in the opposite direction. The colt stopped and stood facing him. "Watch," Joe said. "He'll stop his cavorting and watch me. He's not about to let me pet 'im. That'll come later."

Time and again, Joe repeated the bag trick. Each time, the colt stopped his huffing and watched Joe with the white bag over his head.

"Smart, hadn't thought of that," Claudia said, still puzzled that the trick seemed to work.

"When he'll watch me, I know I have his attention. Then I'll go to other tricks." How well Joe remembered the very same procedure with his horse Rusty. How in time they'd connected so well. "Horses have a lot of sense," he commented. "They have to learn to trust us, know that we don't intend to hurt them. Predators give them a hard time in the wild, and you realize, Claudia, they've bred in the wild for years—since the Spanish explorers left them behind years ago." Joe had read it in a magazine while still in school in Oklahoma.

"You seem to know your history, Joe. I guess I'd forgotten all that."

For the next two hours, Joe worked with the colt, waiting patiently while it ran repeatedly away and around in circles. The colt stopped and watched for a few seconds, then spurted off into a gallop. Joe knew if he could get his attention, he'd step closer to make eye contact, but it'd take patience and persistence before he could hope for a connection so intimate.

"What's the colt's name?" he asked Claudia, who still watched at the sidelines.

"I'm letting Roslynn—that's my godchild—name 'im herself. I thought she'd like it that way."

"How old did you say she is? The girl?"

"Thirteen next week. The colt is to be her birthday gift... gift into the teens." Claudia smiled proudly. "She's wanted a horse for ages, I think since she's been able to get on one."

"Just make sure nobody beats or spooks the colt. He's nervous enough as it is. I never hit a horse while I'm working with one... or any other time, really. It don't pay."

"I can tell you know your business, Joe. This mustang is gonna be your project," Claudia said with emphasis.

Joe's spirits soared. Self-confidence was one thing he was short on, and Claudia seemed to know just what to say to remedy it.

After a while with the mustang Joe said, "Could I see the thoroughbreds?"

"Sure, come with me. In fact, High Pockets needs some exercise. Want to ride 'im?"

Joe grinned. "Be glad to." Every cell in his body exploded!

"I'm planning to find a trainer for 'im soon and get 'im into racing."

Again, Joe grinned and nodded as he followed her to a second corral at the other side of the stables. When she opened the gate, the animals came toward them. Joe extended his hand to rub High Pockets's smooth coat that shone in the sunlight. The colt appeared strong and well developed. "Good boy," Joe said. "Pretty boy. Looks like you have some good blood here… a winner."

"I hope so. You can breeze 'im along the trail there." She motioned. "See what you think of my prize boy." Claudia smiled exuberantly. "I expect great things out of this horse… get 'im into the races, big stakes races." Her blue eyes danced as she handed him the reins.

"I'll bet… big money, too."

"And get the best jockey ever." Her eyes widened.

Joe put the saddle on the horse and soon pulled his small frame into the irons and over the mount's back. With his knees up close to High Pockets's shoulders, he sped down the trail with the sun in his face and the freshness of success spewing from every ounce of his small body!

CHAPTER 9

"WHEN WILL I GET to ride Rascal?" Roslynn asked, referring to the mustang. She'd come after school a lot since the first of March.

"He's coming around. I've taken a few spills off 'im, but you'd better wait a little longer," Joe cautioned. He liked having Roslynn at the ranch; in some ways she reminded him of Jessie. Jessie was three years older than he, and his sister didn't resemble Roslynn at all; she was a blonde. But it was the way girls act so helpless, he guessed, and he could tell that Roslynn already looked up to him. "Come, boy," he said as he opened the corral gate to approach the colt.

"But it's been two months already," Roslynn whined. "Never thought it'd take this long."

"Takes patience. Can't rush these wild mustangs. They've had their way on the plains too long."

"Come, boy," Roslynn petted and extended her hand, but frowned when the colt turned, neighed, and jerked away. "He's afraid of me." Her expression fell as her hair blew into her downcast face.

Joe called to Rascal and the colt stopped. "What you need to do is to let me put the bridle on 'im and you lead him along the fence. He can't get out, and he needs to learn to recognize your voice, your presence. He'll get used to you that way."

Rosalynn smiled at the idea and took the reins.

Joe grinned proudly when it seemed he had made his point. He liked to impress Roslynn, show how much he knew about horses. She was always asking his advice. She jumped, startled, when the colt abruptly reared with a whinny, broke loose, and ran like crazy about the corral. The girl stood terrified, wringing her hands and yelling, "He won't let me lead him."

"Don't give up," Joe consoled and stepped toward the colt to slow him. It was obvious that the horse recognized his voice and obeyed. Joe proudly picked up the reins with a grin out the corner of his mouth, his blond, sun-streaked hair blowing into his sweaty face, and with a command, the colt halted and stood staring at him. "These ponies have no limits in the wild. They run their fool selves all over the place. Rascal will come around. Just give 'im time." It was obvious that Roslynn was growing impatient.

She watched with an envious glare as Joe worked with the colt. Ordinarily, she wasn't so quiet. Afternoons after school was her time to cut loose, humming, prancing, or telling some gosh-awful joke. Joe pretended to ignore a lot of it, but deep down he enjoyed her frivolous ways... someone on his own level.

"Joe." It was Chub Huskerly, Claudia's new trainer. He was fulltime help now and had moved into the guest cottage behind the big house.

"Comin'," Joe replied and turned to Roslynn. "I have to go help Chub. Do you want to have another try at leading your colt?"

"Not today. Tomorrow, probably," and with that she disappeared into the house. He took the bridle off the colt and went to find Chub.

Chub Huskerly was a man of medium build, muscular shoulders, and strong legs. His wide, friendly face, framed by a crew cut, made him appear younger than his actual age; Claudia had mentioned that he was forty-three, and to say that he knew horses was the understatement of the year. Born and reared somewhere back east—Virginia or Maryland—he had grown up under the tutorage of his father who trained some of the best thoroughbreds in the country.

Joe liked Chub, well, most of the time. The outgoing man, so confident in his knowledge of horses and racing, sometimes seemed overbearing, intimidating... at least in Joe's opinion. Because Joe was spending over half of his time at the ranch (Claudia had arranged the tack shop to accommodate a cot, thirteen-inch TV, and a small refrigerator), it seemed reasonable that he'd have to consider Chub his boss; he'd have to shape up. And, the new arrangement sure beat the two-mile walk into town each afternoon. If it hadn't been for the question of school attendance, he would have made the tack shop his fulltime home. Strange, though, Claudia had failed to mention the permission slip. Whether she'd forgotten or half suspected that he wasn't enrolled in school was anybody's guess. She didn't ask and he didn't tell. The important part was she liked him, had given him a lot of responsibility with her horses—that is, up until Chub came, and then everything changed; suddenly, everything had to go Chub's way. He was there to train High Pockets, her prize thoroughbred, soon to turn two, and nothing else mattered... it was obvious. He could see her point, though, with the high price Ted had paid for the colt, and it was true that with the colt's good bloodline and strong physical features, there was reason to doubt good results, especially with the right trainer. Joe knew he had to succumb to Chub's instructions or leave, and he wasn't about to leave Whispering Trails. If Chub got too pushy, Joe usually pretended to have business or a headache and would sulk away into town to sleep at Miss Lily's where he had rented a ten-dollar per night room. The old woman seldom knew when he was on the place, unless it was time to pay up. Both he and she liked it that way. With a weekly salary, he could afford it.

"Joe." It was Chub again.

"Be right there." He dashed out to see what the new trainer had in mind.

At the big barn, he saw him, face flushed and snarled. Joe cringed. He knew Chub had inspected the stables and wasn't pleased.

"Why didn't you throw down dry litter in the stables?" Chub snapped. "You have to, Joe. If a horse stands in moisture several hours, it'll get hoof rot." Chub didn't look up.

"I wasn't aware of it," Joe complied and stepped to a nearby bin for dry straw.

"And make sure you add a handful of bran to the grain each feeding time," Chub went on to say. "If you're gonna be groom here, do it right." Again, Chub's face twisted into a frown.

Joe didn't comment. What could he say? Claudia had given Chub full charge. "Yes, sir," Joe snapped in compliance.

"You're gonna have to quit spending so much time with that little gal out there and concentrate on your work."

"Roslynn, you mean?"

Chub didn't honor his question.

"Claudia hired me to train the mustang. It's to be Roslynn's riding horse," Joe mumbled, afraid to say more.

Again, Chub didn't answer.

"She's dying to ride the colt, but I told her to wait. The colt's not ready. He'll obey me, but she's still a stranger to 'im." Joe got quiet, afraid Chub was about to ask where he'd learned to train mustangs.

"The mustang can wait. These thoroughbreds come first. They'll need bathing every day, and exercise. If a colt is to get anywhere in the racing world, its training must start early." Chub pursed his lips to emphasize his point. A stern look broke over his face.

"Yes, sir," Joe said in the hope that he'd win Chub's confidence.

"And there are plenty of do's and don't's," Chub added. It's an absolute must that the proper amount of food and water are available." He picked up a curry comb and said, "And look, use a tail comb for the mane and tail. They're the graceful areas of a horse. Really do 'em right, pretty. Adds to the appearance."

Joe watched to see what Chub had in mind.

"Ever used a hoof pick?" Chub picked one up to demonstrate. "It moves small objects from the feet. Little tricks of the trade make all the difference in a race horse."

Joe realized he'd never heard so many pointers. For several minutes, Chub went over all aspects of grooming—brushing the hair in the direction that it grew with a special brushing in the hock depressions and a careful examination of any changes such as cuts, lumps, or scratches. "You must learn to do it right or not at all, young man. Mrs. McClish will tolerate nothing less and neither will I." Chub looked at Joe with a glare.

Joe secretly bristled, wanting to spit in Chub's face, but he also realized that Chub knew horses and anything he learned from the top-notched trainer would be to his advantage.

It was getting dark when Chub finished, and to say that Joe was weary of his presence was putting it mildly... the two-mile stroll into town would seem like a respite. He'd finished his chores, anyway, and Chub was closing up for the night. No reason to hang around. Whether his efforts had come up to Chub's standards, he'd probably hear about it later. For now, he wanted to disappear, get away!

As he left, he saw the new trainer pull Claudia's pickup into the garage down by the barn. "That dude thinks he owns this place," Joe muttered, seething with disgust as he hurried along to Miss Lily's.

CHAPTER 10

ARLY MARCH BROUGHT WARMER days to Pittsburgh; weather warm
enough for classes on the terrace. By all accounts, school for Persia
was progressing as expected. Time had flown since the accident, even
with Bebe still in Florida. Classmates from school had helped to fill the
gap. Molly Mosier, Persia's closest friend, called daily, and several times
they'd met after school for Cokes. Molly was on the cheerleading squad
and knew all the scoop at school.

Mr. Elgard, even with his gauche demeanor, seemed more casual,
too. His astuteness impressed her. Their lengthy delves into novels and
history made it all come alive, sometimes lasting the entire morning.
One aspect of him that she particularly liked was his willingness to
allow her to disagree; like when she blurted her own opinion. At such
times, he'd merely readjust his glasses and focus his small intense eyes
into hers.

"Let's discuss chapters one and two tomorrow," he said that morning at the end of the session. "Unless you have further questions, we'll consider it a day." He shuffled his papers and prepared to leave.

Persia closed her books and said goodbye at the foot of the stairs. In the kitchen, Maud asked, "Has he gone?"

"He always leaves at noon. What's for lunch?"

"A chicken breast with mushrooms… a salad, too, if you like."

"Fix it all, please. I'm starved… a big sandwich, too."

Persia pulled out a chair at a small kitchen table and waited. "Maud," she began, somewhat perplexed, "spring break comes up in two weeks. Do you think Bebe will let me go?"

"Oh, child, you'll have to ask him. With the school kids I assume." She took the mushrooms from the refrigerator.

"Yes. My senior class. They're going to the Caribbean. Don't ask me where down there." Persia found a wisp of her hair and began to twist it. "I'll have to ask Molly."

"You'll have to go to your dad with that." Maud pursed her lips. "By the way, when do you expect 'im?"

"Not sure. He seems in no hurry to get back." Persia frowned. "He hasn't even told me how he feels—his back."

"He will in time. Some men are reluctant to discuss health problems. I guess they think it's weak or not macho." She rolled her eyes.

"Guess so. I do miss 'im, though, especially with Mumsy gone." The sad feeling returned. "I miss her."

"Yeah, your mom was some woman. He'll be hard put to find another like her."

"You talk like you think he's dating already." Persia grimaced. "What kind of respect is that?"

"Not to imply that at all," Maud said. "But, child, men will be men."

"And he'll get plenty of crap outta me if he is," Persia snapped in a raised voice. "Mumsy's been dead less than three months."

Maud set the food before her and soon disappeared down the hall.

* * * *　* * * *　* * * *

"Persia." It was B. W. on the phone that evening. "How's school? Are you doing your homework, and how about your memory exercises?"

"Yep, every day. Where are you? You sound so far away."

"In Florida still. Just wanted to check on you. Does your head ache?"

"Not lately," she began. "School's going fine, too. I made an A on my literature exam last week."

"And your memory? Is it better?"

"Somewhat. Just the early things. I still can't remember my first grade teacher's name or where I went to school... if that matters. Dr. Brody said it'd take a while."

"Yes, but do continue to work at it. You must, baby."

"I know, but there's something I need to ask you. Spring break is coming up in two weeks," she began changing the subject. "My classmates want me to go with them. Can I? They're going to the Caribbean."

"Where in the Caribbean?"

"Don't know." She waited for his response.

"Baby, I'm gonna have to say no—not to disappoint you, but I can't risk another family loss. I just lost Claire, you know." His voice cracked the way it always did at the mention of her name.

"Lose me? How do you figure that? Chaperones will go. Besides, Bebe, I'm eighteen now."

"But things get wild at those events. I know how they party. Any parent would be hard put to allow something such as that." His voice sounded firm and deliberate.

"Hawh, dad"—she'd never referred to him as dad—"that's ridiculous. I'm not a baby anymore."

"I know, but wait. I have a surprise."

"A surprise?"

"Next month I'm planning a business meeting at Hilton Head in South Carolina. It's to end with a reception at Beaufort. I need to show some life about me. They may think I'm dead or something." He chuckled.

"Reception?" She repeated. She knew absolutely nothing of his business ventures.

"Hilton Head is such a popular resort, good golfing and location. The staff will love it. Wanna come?"

"You've not changed, I see. It's still golf." She hesitated. "Where is this place?"

"Between Charlestown and Savannah. A friend told me that Beaufort was the perfect spot for a party. It's not far from Hilton Head—old southern mansions, live oaks, Spanish moss—that kind of thing. You need to come, baby, help me entertain; I want to show you off."

"When is it?"

"The second weekend in April. You'd come down on the company jet. In fact, I'll ask Jeff Lorton to pick you up at the house. You two can fly into Savannah and rent a car."

"Do you know him? Not some old codger, I hope."

"No, he just graduated from the University. Very bright young man and has his MBA. He's our new field rep there... all the northwest region of the state."

"I'll think about it." How dull, she thought, but couldn't dare say it. "But spring break comes before that. Why couldn't I plan on both? It's my last year of school, Bebe. Can't you understand?"

"I've expressed myself already, Persia. I'm concerned for your safety. You don't need the kind of exposure that you might get there... the rougher element. Besides, you're not completely recovered."

She knew B. W. Plemons—a kind man all right, empathetic, too, and warm. But with all his good human qualities, he'd developed into one heck of a businessman... educated, cool under pressure, and shrewd. When he made up his mind there was little or no negotiating. "So when will I see you?" she mumbled, seething.

"In a few weeks."

"Okay," she managed to say and angrily threw down the telephone. "The very idea," she squawked, livid that he'd nixed the trip. "If Mumsy were here, she's make 'im let me go. He'd listen to her."

* * * * * * * * * *

Mr. Elgard must have noticed her pouty expression. The next morning, he began class with a corny little joke. Persia listened with a smirk, but managed to brighten into a smile when it was obvious that her tutor was hurt, embarrassed at her indifference. A few seconds later, he composed himself, ready to begin class. Still disgruntled with her dad's decision, she commented little until Mr. Elgard announced his latest assignment—a research paper of at least two-thousand words on any phase of science. At that, she sat up and blurted, "Why do I have to do that I don't plan on a scientific career."

He glared at her and replied, "How do you know at this point? Every university in the country requires good writing skills."

"In science?"

"In any subject, and we haven't stressed science at all this semester. Your dad's in the oil business; I thought you'd jump at the chance to delve into something different… something pertaining to oil, perhaps."

"I don't care about his business. Right this minute, I could care less about him. He makes me plenty angry at times."

Whatever Mr. Elgard thought he didn't say, only smirked and readjusted his glasses. "Let's make it due by May 1st, two weeks before graduation."

Assignments in history and social studies filled the next two hours… the Battle of Shiloh in history, and the pros and cons of the Carter Administration in social studies, all of which helped to alleviate her stress.

"I take it you're not happy today," Mr. Elgard said as he prepared to leave.

"It's my dad. He won't allow me to go with my class spring break."

"I see," was his curt remark at the door. "See ya tomorrow."

"Baby." It was B. W. again that evening. "I've done some thinking. I guess I was a little too over-protective last night… the Caribbean trip."

"I thought so. Can I go?"

"I've decided to let you go."

"You have?" she squealed.

"Yeah, provided you'll stay with your friends and provided you'll come to Beaufort for me. You will, won't you?"

"Why, uh, sure, I guess so."

"It's important to me, dear. I have someone I want you to meet."

"A boyfriend? You've found me a boyfriend?" She giggled.

"My lady friend, Sheri Tahlwald."

"Oh." Her voice dropped like lead. "So you *are* dating someone?"

He didn't comment. "Go ahead and plan the Caribbean trip."

There was little else to say except, "Thanks, Dad."

CHAPTER 11

"Molly," Persia squealed into the telephone the next day. "My dad says I can go—go with the class. He finally gave in."

"He did. Great! I thought he'd come around. We're gonna have one big blast! I can't wait. Can you?"

"Did you tell the others?"

"No, but I will. It wouldn't be the same without you, girl. I'm thrilled," Molly said in her usual giddy manner. Molly was voted Miss Congeniality at last year's homecoming; everybody liked her. Now, to get on with the plans… shopping especially.

* * * * * * * * * * * *

The following two weeks were busy—much too busy to spend time with the gang, except for a couple of afternoons with Molly to finalize plans for the trip. But planning wasn't all; more than ever, she poured herself into her studies. Bebe was right; it was time to set her sights on college. At least three afternoons she'd spent in the library to study her options for the research paper, and more than once, she'd gone to read additional historical accounts of Civil War battles for extra credit in history. Mr. Elgard must have noticed; he joked more, seemed more relaxed, even bought new glasses!

"You be careful down there, now," he said on the day before vacation. "Don't let those islanders fast talk ya." A broad grin broke across his angular face as he gave a thumbs-up sign on his way out. Even his dry sense of humor sometimes amused her.

"Don't worry. I'll come back as tan as a biscuit," she replied, glowing with anticipation.

* * * *   * * * *   * * * *

The flight captain announced the descent as they approached the resort of Luceta on the northern shore of Jamaica. From the plane's window, she saw white sandy beaches and the ocean, blue and shimmering. The resort appeared small, consisting mostly of hotels, clubs, and restaurants, which in the tropical sunlight resembled a French painting.

"Where are we to stay?" Persia turned to Molly and asked. "Our hotel?"

"The Shoreline. We should have a great view, too. I can't wait." Molly's eyes glowed with glee.

"I know," Persia replied, already thrilled at the prospects.

When the plane landed and the class was about to disembark, someone yelled, "Let's hit the beach!" Others clamored toward arcades to play the games.

"Kids, hotel first," Mrs. McKay, acting as chaperone, yelled. "We have to check in before anything else." She assembled them and entered the hotel.

The check-in took mere minutes after which Persia and Molly sped to their room on the third floor to change.

"Take a look at this view," Molly squealed as she stood and looked out over the water. "Have you ever seen anything so pretty?"

"Yeah, if only we had a date," Persia kidded. "Let's change into our swimsuits and head for the beach." She began to undress. "And grab a bite of lunch on the way."

With beach towels and suntan oil in hand, they rushed to join the crowd already cavorting on the beach where tourists and natives mingled, sang, shouted boisterously together like a bunch of wild turkeys at feeding time.

"Have you ever seen so many good-looking hunks?" Molly whispered as she scanned the crowd. "People from everywhere."

"And look at this one coming here," Persia added… that tan and those legs." A male, suntanned and lean, came toward them.

"And that face!"

"Hi," he greeted and plopped down beside them. "On vacation?" His dark eyes had a lustful lure to them. "What's your name? I'm Eddy."

"I'm Persia and she's Molly. It's spring break."

"Where you from?"

"Pittsburgh, and you?"

"Houston. Been here before?"

"Nope, first time. Say you're from Houston?" Molly asked as she sized him up—good looking, for sure, a little cocky, though, even spoke with a slight accent. Bet he pumps iron, too, she thought, impressed with his muscular physique.

"You in school there? In Texas?" Persia asked.

"Already graduated. I'm twenty."

"Oh, old man, huh?"

"Wanna Coke anybody?" Molly asked and stood.

"Not now, thanks."

"Not me," Eddy replied, his eyes on Persia. "Wanna dance?"

"Sure." Her heart raced at the chance. Eddy was cool.

With that, he pulled her up and led her into a series of gyrations synchronized to the beat, often pulling her to him in sensuous maneuvers.

"Some dancer you are. I take it you're not new here," Persia said as she danced.

"Been here a few times." He glanced away. "What do you do in Pittsburgh?"

"I'm still in school."

"Eighteen yet?"

"Since last November."

For several seconds neither spoke. In their bare feet, they moved to the beat with an occasional twirl or dip that resulted in intimate touches, something she hadn't expected. Surprised, she cringed. What did he mean by such aggressive behavior?

"I'd better join my friend," she said and quickly dashed over to where Molly sat sipping Coke.

"Some hunk, I'd say," Molly whispered when Persia joined her. "Those abs are to die for."

"And the accent. Do you think he's really from Texas?"

"Who knows. He's working the crowd... too fresh for me." Persia giggled frivolously and decided on a Coke. It was hot.

That evening when the class assembled for dinner, Mrs. McKay repeated the liquor rules. Only those who were eighteen could imbibe with a limit of two drinks.

The strip, a conglomerate of shops, clubs, and restaurants with their neon lights to beckon tourists, was crowded. Hordes of people mingled like ants with curious expectations… fun at any cost! It was time to party!

At the Joilé Club, Persia and Molly entered, and soon a waiter approached to take their order. "Sodas, please," they mumbled cautiously. "Where is Mrs. McKay? I'm dying to try a martini," Molly whispered. "They're so sophisticated. Movie stars always have martinis."

"Are they gin or vodka?"

"Don't ask me. But as sure as I order one, Mrs. McKay will walk right through that door," Molly murmured. "I'm not eighteen yet."

"I don't think she's here," Persia insisted as she scanned the crowd. "You could always put it under the table if she came."

"Hey, Persia, look who's there… it's your guy again."

Persia craned to see. "Oh my gosh, the hunk again and two of his friends." She rolled her eyes.

"They're not with dates, either."

"Oh gosh, they've spotted us. Here they come."

"Let's pretend we don't see them."

"Why?"

"We can't appear to be too anxious," Persia whispered.

"Hi, remember me?" Eddy said. "Meet my friends. This is Toby, and he's Josh." He motioned. "This is Persia that I told you about earlier and her friend."

"Molly. Her name is *Molly*," Persia explained.

"Hi," they said. "Okay if we join ya?" Eddy asked, and pulled out a chair.

"Guess so," Molly muttered. "Enjoying your vacation? You *are* from Houston, you said."

Eddy got a strange look and grinned sheepishly toward his friends.

For the next few minutes, the five of them sat chatting and laughing with one crazy comment after another until finally Eddy invited Persia to dance.

Flippantly, she arose as they made their way to the crowded floor.

"You drinkin'?" he asked once they'd begun.

"A soda is all."

"That's no fun."

"I'm having fun." She glared at him.

"Don't be so touchy," he whispered and drew her to him. "Has anyone ever told you how beautiful you are?" He brushed her cheek with his lips when a romantic Elvis tune began. For the next few moments, he held her close, their bodies moving in sensuous harmony. "Walk out on the beach with me," he whispered. "The moon is out."

"I can't—can't leave my friend. I'm with her."

"You tied to her or something? She might not even miss us."

"Can't," Persia repeated and broke from him to join Molly.

Apparently irritated, he said to his friends "Come on, let's go."

* * * *   * * * *   * * * *

Spring break was rapidly coming to an end; it was Thursday already and thoughts of returning to ho-hum schoolwork were on everyone's mind. By eight that evening, "one last fling," as Persia put it, was the goal of the day, and no better place than Joilé Club where a celebratory atmosphere already prevailed. Music and boisterous voices mixed in chaotic fashion. She and Molly joined classmates for the last chance to party!

"It's so crowded here it's difficult to find space on the dance floor," Persia complained as they settled at a table near the front. "Have you ever seen so many people?"

"I guess we can always tell our kids that we survived spring break," Molly kidded.

"Yeah. Look, Molly, there's our friend Eddy already here. Just arrived, it looks like, and he's alone this time."

They watched as he stepped to the bar where he took a stool and began to chat with Dave, the bartender. "He's one cool guy, if you ask me," Molly whispered.

"Yep, but you know what? I think he knows it."

"I think he has a thing for you?"

"I don't know why. Well," Persia continued, "he did ask me to go for a walk on the beach last Tuesday night. Did I tell ya?"

"He did? But look, girl, don't get too hung up on 'im. We're to go home tomorrow, you know. Romances don't last by long distance."

"I know. Just a whim. I've read that vacations aren't complete unless a romance blossoms." Persia sighed. "At least that's how romance novels put it."

"You're such a romantic," Molly said just as Lee Swain stepped up to ask her to dance. Lee had escorted her to the prom the year before.

Persia watched them step onto the floor, then glanced again toward the bar where Eddy sat. Summing him up, somehow, something about the guy didn't add up. He *was* a rave—possessed enough charm for six, but sly or was it mysterious?

The urge hit! The restroom, where? In a narrow hallway just beyond the bar a sign read *Women*. While Molly danced with Lee, she'd slip among the crowd and return before Molly and Lee finished the dance.

"Hi," Eddy said and turned just as she approached the bar. "Where's your friend? Come have a drink with me."

"She's dancing." She hesitated and glanced about for Mrs. McKay. I'm eighteen, she told herself. What the heck? Vacation is ending. Why not? "Sure, think I will; make it a martini and dry." She watched his expression. Had she said it correctly? She'd never had a martini.

"I'm on my way back here," she said and motioned toward the restroom. "Be back in a minute."

Later, at the bar, they chatted for a time with the bartender before Eddy insisted they dance. The martini had hit like a grenade, and if she'd ever felt stranger, she couldn't remember it. "Sure, let's do," she giggled and followed him out to the floor. "There's Molly and Lee over there. Let's show them a step or two."

He looked at her strangely, as if he'd noticed her incoherence. "Wait here; I'll be right back. Gotta see the bartender a minute." He skipped across the floor and whispered to his friend, Dave.

When he returned, they began the dance, a slow one, something by Barbra Streisand, "You Don't Bring Me Flowers Anymore."

"Who's that singing?" she asked.

"Can't prove it by me, but I like it." He drew her to him and kissed her cheek.

At ease now and wrapped in Eddy's arms, she felt his caress as smooth and warm as milk chocolate, a perfect evening in a perfect place.

Too bad it'd soon end, and to think she'd almost missed the vacation. Luckily, Bebe had changed his mind. "You live in Houston, you say? How far is that from Oklahoma?" she whispered as they danced.

"I thought you were from Pittsburgh." He ignored her question regarding Houston. "You been here before?"

"No, have you?"

"Again, he ignored her question. When the love song ended, he said, "Let's go finish our drinks."

She followed him to the bar, where they took a seat and Eddy and Dave resumed their conversation. "Biggest crowd all year," he said to Dave. She wondered how Eddy would know, but who was she to ask? They soon upped the drinks and Eddy suggested they leave.

"Wanna go for a walk on the beach? The moon is out." It was the same invitation as before.

"Sure, but let me tell Molly first. I'm with her."

Eddy frowned as if irritated. "We're adults. Why ask her?"

She looked about to see Molly but saw nothing of her.

Outside, he said, "Let's go this way." He directed and led her along a back way some distance from the water. A few plants and structures obscured the path; lighting was dim. Suddenly, he stopped and yanked her to him, then kissed her savagely. "Take off your clothes," he demanded.

Already dizzy, Persia swerved away from him. "Stop!" she yelled. Her head spun and her knees shook. "Stop it, Eddy."

"I said take off your clothes."

"No, I'll scream."

"Go ahead, woman. Nobody would ever hear you out here."

"Stop. Let me go." So this is his idea of a walk on the beach.

"Shut up and pull off your clothes. Unbutton your top." His hands felt rough to her skin.

"Rape is a crime," she moaned before falling to the sand. "Stop it now, you idiot. Let me go. You have no right to—"

"Lie down." He slapped her face.

"No."

"I said lie down."

Bewildered, she managed to hobble away and sit up behind a clump of sea grass. With her hands, she covered her bare breasts as she drifted in and out of consciousness. She couldn't think; she couldn't speak. A dark blur came over her. A dim outline of his body moved about her. She managed to scream, "Help," before he forced her onto the sand. "Help me, please," she screamed and then fell unconscious.

A couple of minutes passed before a light suddenly flashed behind them. Had Toby and the other friend of his… who was he, anyway? Had they come to join him? Had Eddy planned a date-rape?

The light appeared closer. He got up and with a dash suddenly disappeared into the darkness! She couldn't tell where or when, but heard voices.

"Persia, where are you?" The voice soon faded. The light came closer. "Persia, please answer." She could say nothing, already in a stupor with the wind in her face and sand in her eyes.

* * * * * * * * * *

The next day at the island hospital, Molly and Mrs. McKay came to check. Persia, awake now but sore and bruised, lay motionless. The shame for her poor judgment gave her a headache.

"Mrs. McKay, I know you want to kill me for disregarding the rules. That guy must've slipped something into my drink."

"I guess you won't do this again," was Mrs. McKay's only remark. "But look, we've notified your dad and he's sending the company plane down for you... be here this afternoon. The class will leave now in a short time. Are you okay? I mean, thinking clearly?"

"Yes, and I'm sure my dad will be furious with me."

"Well, don't concentrate on it now. Just get well and get home. Some young man by the name of Jeff Lorton is to come for you."

"Yes, ma'am," was all she could say. Too much had happened already.

CHAPTER 12

WHEN JEFF LORTON ARRIVED that afternoon and found her sitting in the hospital room with her bag already packed, he introduced himself, grinned, and said, "I guess you're ready to go home." He was handsome enough; eyes as blue as a button-down oxford shirt, and a dazzling white smile that indicated a pleasing personality.

"More than ready," she muttered, weary from the wait. She allowed him to take her bag for the trip out front.

"Are you walking, or do I need to get a wheelchair?"

"I can walk, thanks. I've already checked out with the business office."

"You're sure? You're rather banged up. Did you have an accident?" It was obvious that B. W. hadn't explained the trip to him.

Timidly, she tucked her chin, embarrassed, and said, "Did something stupid."

He studied her strangely.

"No, it was an attempted date-rape. Ever hear the term 'slippin' a mickie'?" She managed a half smile. "That's what happened."

"You're kidding. My gosh, how did you escape?" His face had horror written all over it. "I'm surprised you lived to tell about it."

"My friend, Molly Mosier, missed me at the club where we were and came looking for me. When she didn't find me, she called the police. I reckon they arrested the SOB. Wasn't conscious at the time, but came to at the ER."

Jeff stared in disbelief. "I've heard of such but have never known it to happen in real life—the movies, maybe."

"It was my fault. I acted stupid, naïve, but I'll know next time." She rolled her eyes. "I do appreciate your trip down to get me. I guess you think you're doing double duty."

"No sweat, better than writing up leases." His boyish face cracked into a grin.

"Is that what you do at Wesco?"

"Mineral rights and leases," he said as they boarded the plane.

* * * * * * * * * *

At the airport in Pittsburgh, he hailed a cab for Clairmont and later at the front door set her bag inside.

"Thanks for the rescue," she said and smiled. "I feel terrible at being so much trouble." She made eye contact and saw a caring expression. "You're so kind."

"Just glad to help," he replied and smiled.

"And look, Mr. Lorton," she said, "please don't tell my dad how bruised I am. He—"

"I'll let you do the explaining, but please do me a favor. Drop the *Mister Lorton* stuff. I'm Jeff, okay?"

"Okay," she murmured and watched him step back to the cab.

* * * *   * * * *   * * * *

The weekend passed calmly enough. After a brief explanation to Maud and the expected telephone call—tongue-lashing—from her dad, she retired to her quarters upstairs hoping to shut out the world. Depressed and out of sorts, she wanted to see no one, and to think that Mr. Elgard would expect her undivided attention in class Monday morning was more than she wanted to think of at the moment.

* * * *   * * * *   * * * *

"You're not tan, you're purple," he teased when he arrived for class Monday morning. "What happened?"

Caught off guard, Persia glanced away, rearranged her papers, and pretended to ignore him.

"Have a wreck?" His angular face seemed thinner than usual, and his beady eyes pierced straight into hers.

"Guess you could call it that," she finally said. "A physical one." She opened her history book to the *Battle of Vicksburg*. "Got attacked," she mumbled. "By a stranger."

"In Jamaica?"

"Yep. Luckily, I escaped. It was plenty darn scary, though. Don't make me rehash the details, please." Whether it was repression or a memory loss, she remembered few of the details, anyway.

Awkwardly, he began the assignment. "Now that we have only two months of school remaining, how is your research paper progressing? Have you decided on a topic?"

"I've done some reading, gone to the library three or four times. How many words did you say?"

"At least two-thousand. I'd make an outline first, followed by a synopsis as a guide. You'll do better that way. Now to history... the Battle of Vicksburg."

With her book already open, she waited for him to start the discussion. History was a favorite of his; if she knew him, he'd begin and ramble on for the entire two hours, which suited her. She had other items on her mind; a gift for Molly, who saved her life, and Mrs. McKay had called over the weekend to make sure she'd arrived home safely; reminded her, too, that the prom was a mere two weeks away. "Do come," Mrs. McKay said. "Bring anyone you wish," to which Persia had graciously declined, embarrassed at the commotion she'd caused on the trip. All she wanted now was to pour herself into her books and graduate. But, well, there was that darn trip to South Carolina—Beaufort! If only she could connive herself out of that one—where *was* Beaufort, anyway?

* * * *   * * * *   * * * *

The first week home from spring break was a breeze; aced a couple of exams! The second week wasn't as busy; she'd focused on some of the options for the research paper. Somehow, she kept shoving it aside, halfway hoping that Mr. Girard might change his mind. When Molly called insisting that they enjoy an afternoon out, she jumped at the chance. A visit to the downtown strip hinted of fun, and she was game; she was beginning to feel normal again!

By the third week in April, anxiety overwhelmed her; the trip to South Carolina was at hand. Disgruntled at her lack of excuses, she teetered on the idea of merely calling her dad to say she couldn't make it. On the other hand, he was livid already, and to make life more miserable was out of the question. She'd go to Beaufort and make the best of it. I'm eighteen now, she told herself. I'll soon graduate, and I can do as

I please. What Bebe does—with that Sherri Tahlwald—is up to him. Mumsy's gone. Life here will never be the same.

Suddenly, everything turned dark, uncertain, as she stood before the wide window in her room and looked down. Even the lush gardens, radiant in spring color, didn't dispel the gloom. If Mumsy were here, she could hold my hand and reassure me that life sometimes seems dark, but somewhere there's a brighter side... "Mumsy, I miss you," she whispered, her eyes full of tears. "Miss you more than I can ever say. Why didn't I tell you more often how much I loved you? Seems like Bebe never spends time with me anymore," she sobbed, broken hearted.

CHAPTER 13

THE SMALL TOWN OF Beaufort was located between Savannah and Charleston in the lowcountry of South Carolina.

Two weeks later, she and Jeff Lorton—again, B. W. had assigned him to escort his daughter down—headed north out to Savannah. Unsure as to the route, Persia opened a leather briefcase for a map.

"Hilton Head is south of Beaufort," she said, running a finger along the highway going north. "Is that correct?"

"I guess so. You're the navigator," he commented with a boyish chuckle as he watched the traffic ahead.

"In that case, we may get lost," she teased. Surprisingly, his bubbly personality had buoyed her spirits. He was fun; had a wry sense of humor.

"Would that be so bad—getting lost with a beautiful woman?" He gave her a flashy flirtatious grin.

"Silly." She winked.

"This really is low country. Bet they have all kinds of seafood down here. Have you tried soft-shelled crab?" he asked.

"Can't say that I have. Is it good?"

"Terrific... my favorite." He hesitated a moment. "What's this place called that I'm to drop you off... or deliver you?" Again, he grinned. "Dispose of you." He chuckled.

"Come off it. It's Scarlett's Parlor, a bed and breakfast. Sound Southern?"

"Just a little."

At the next intersection, he turned right and followed the street into the historic district of Beaufort, as charming as an old poster she remembered of Tara in *Gone with the Wind*.

"My gosh," Persia gasped when Jeff located the address and turned into the driveway. "What is this lady's name?" She began to shuffle papers. "Gracie Patterson, it says here. Yeah, that's it."

He stopped the car and they got out. "Got everything? I'll get your bag," he said. "Some place this is. Look at that tree."

"Live oak. Bet it's a hundred years old." She stopped to study the house's façade... a work of art, for sure. Three levels it was, each with a balcony or porch surrounded by a rail. Wicker furniture, too, and those lush Boston ferns. Picture perfect, she thought as she rang the doorbell and waited to meet Gracie Patterson.

Gracie was a short, stout-looking woman with dark hair pulled back to accent a jolly face with *welcome* written all over it.

"I'm Persia Plemons."

"Yes, Miss Plemons. I expected you. Won't you come in. I'm

Gracie... just call me Gracie, no *ma'am* stuff." She smiled and extended her hand.

"And this is Jeff Lorton, who accompanied me," Persia explained. "He's to leave soon for Hilton Head to join my dad and his employees. I assume Dad made reservations."

"Yes, and you may have your choice, upstairs or down. He reserved three rooms."

Persia stared at her with question... three rooms? Why three rooms? "Yes," she commented as Gracie interrupted.

"And as for tomorrow evening, he told me, or rather he and the lady with him, exactly what they wanted—food for the number to attend, kinds of food, even to the music... a pianist to play southern tunes. You can't get more explicit than that. I followed their instructions to the letter. The food is to be catered... well, except the bread. I always bake my own hot rolls. I have a special recipe." A proud smile broke across her face.

"Did Dad go into all that detail himself? He used to leave all that to my mom. Sadly, she's not with us anymore."

"The woman with him wasn't your mother?" Gracie gasped. "I referred to her as '*Mrs. Plemons.*'"

"His secretary, probably," Persia muttered and realized the woman must've been Sherri Tahlwald.

Jeff Lorton soon excused himself to return to Hilton Head as Persia stepped inside to claim her room on the third floor, already peeved that Sherri Tahlwald had made all the arrangements for the upcoming evening.

No point in getting stressed out, she told herself, and stepped out on the balcony to relax. The ante-bellum neighborhood furnished a great view and reminded her of her American history class. How did all those stately mansions escape Sherman's march to the sea? Most of the homes must have existed during that era. She'd ask Mr. Elgard, or better still, ask Gracie.

From the porch swing, she heard a mockingbird, perched high in the oak, as it went through its many imitations of a dozen or more kinds of birds. Somewhere in her past she faintly remembered a mockingbird, but so much of her past escaped her; the connection soon faded. Soon, Jeff Lorton came to mind; he was fun, nice looking, and youthful. Why did Bebe always manage to team her up with him? Did he have ulterior motives? She giggled… not a chance. Jeff'd think me much too young and inexperienced. He must be twenty-four, at least.

From the balcony, she again scanned the neighborhood, awed by the gorgeous old homes and manicured lawns, and wondered who settled Beaufort, how the lavish area had existed so long.

"Ma'am, I have a question," she said when she joined her hostess downstairs. "About all these old mansions. How did this place escape the Civil War? They must have stood during that era."

"I'm Gracie, remember! Legend has it that one of the property owners at the time knew the general… Sherman, that is… and asked him personally not to destroy this area, to surround it, and he did. At least that's the story we get. Yes, most of these houses were built before the war and exist much as they did back then."

Persia's eyes widened. "That's awesome. Sounds logical enough. The man was a friend to General Sherman?"

"That's what we're told. We're proud of it." A wistful look broke across her face. "I guess it represents the South in its glory days."

"It does for sure. Romantic and beautiful."

"And you have to realize that Charleston," Gracie continued," a few miles away, was one of the oldest ports in the States. The early fur trade and rice crops went all the way back to the 1600s… Rice growing was the main crop here for 200 years."

"All the water, I suppose. I'm gonna have to tell my history teacher all this. He's a history buff." She smiled. The subject changed. "Tell me," Persia began, "about the woman who accompanied my dad. What was she like?"

"Nice, pretty, dark hair and eyes and lots of make-up!"

"Is that all?" Persia sat taking it all in.

"Actually, I didn't notice much else that stood out. She seemed to know what she wanted… the take-charge type."

"And Dad, did he comment or give her full reign?"

"Said very little," Gracie quipped with a grin. "Some men had rather relent than pick a fuss."

"Yeah, I know what you mean. You see, my mom was killed last December in a plane crash. I'm afraid this woman is after my dad's money."

"Oh," Gracie muttered as if trying to avoid a family feud. "I make it a habit not to pry. It's bad for business," she quipped.

CHAPTER 14

WHEN PERSIA HEARD THE first notes of Moon River by the pianist, she went downstairs to join the reception. Already, the lower level was decorated for a party! Candles, positioned at various settings, cast a romantic glow, and large arrangements of gladioli and red roses accented strategic areas of interest. The aroma of cinnamon and ginger, not to mention freshly baked yeast rolls, permeated the entire room—certainly enough to activate one's appetite!

Gracie, already poised in a blue frock, expensive in design, that fit snug under a bosom much too ample for her body size, smiled when Persia joined her in the foyer to greet guests. It was obvious that Gracie's fragrance was Channel No. 5—a favorite of women of substance—it had definitely been Mumsy's favorite, and it *did* fit the occasion.

"Here comes your dad now," Gracie whispered as B. W. and Sherri stepped toward the entry.

Persia dreaded the introduction to the woman who obviously had taken her mother's place. Sherri *was* attractive, the dark features that

Gracie described earlier, and yes, she did wear far more makeup than Mumsy ever did. "Less is more," Mumsy always insisted. "Don't overdo it." Obviously, Sherri didn't share that same opinion!

"You made it, I see," B. W. said to his daughter before giving her a hug. "I want you to meet Sherri Tahlwald."

Persia managed to murmur "Hi" before saying, "Yes, Jeff and I had a great trip."

Sherri extended her hand and whispered, "I've heard so much about you." Her dark eyes, mysterious and evasive, hardly made eye contact as she whispered, "You're beautiful. Everything I expected."

"Thanks," Persia said and quickly turned aside to adjust the neckline to her midnight-blue dress that Mumsy always said accented her cobalt-blue eyes. Actually, she and Mumsy shopped for it in New York… just another tug at her heartstrings—and to think Bebe was already involved with another woman. It was enough to make her want to vomit!

After a while, Gracie skillfully directed the guests toward the table set with damask cloth, monogrammed napkins, and more silver than a Colorado silver mine—flatware, tea and coffee service, and the largest chafing dish ever, filled with steaming meatballs! Even Clairmont's ornateness in no way compared. The Old South must've risen again, Persia thought as she moved in to serve herself.

"Don't you look nice." It was Jeff Lorton behind her who whispered over her shoulder. His warm breath on her neck sent a surge of passion like a tsunami moving inland, and he smelled so good!

"How was the meeting," she asked, happy to see him again.

"Business as usual." He forked a couple of meatballs onto his plate. "I'm afraid I won't get to fly home with you tomorrow. I have to leave tonight."

Why?" She turned to face him, surprised.

"A couple of new leases up at New Castle." He continued to help himself to the food.

"Too bad. I'll miss you." She frowned. "Who will take me down to Savannah to the airport?"

"Your dad will work it out. He knows I'm to leave later."

She watched as he settled into a chair on the other side of the room and proceeded to help herself to the food. Occasionally, she glanced toward her dad and Sherri, who sat across the room with their heads together like two teens after the prom. Suddenly, her appetite waned, as she determined not to go anywhere near them. Instead, she seated herself near a young man who introduced himself as Reid Morgan of Charleston, who grinned as she approached.

"Are you with Wesco, too?" she asked and noticed his lawyer-like style; neat and suave.

"No, I'm afraid B. W. found me on the golf course and insisted I come." He hesitated as though waiting for her comment. "I'm a research scientist in Charleston."

"You are. On what?" Scientist? What a twist. Certainly different, to say the least.

"The horseshoe crab. We've found a factor in its blood that's interesting—holds promise for curing disease." His eyes, darker than most, reflected a mental acuteness that made her take notice.

"You mean such as the crabs found in this area? A plain old crab?"

He laughed. "Sure. Ever seen a horseshoe crab? They resemble a horse's foot."

"And what's so special about it?"

"Its blood. It has blue blood instead of red."

"You're kidding." She stared at him curiously.

"But my work is involved in the isolation of the factor that I mentioned to see if it combines with certain bacteria to cause clotting."

"You've lost me already, but it does sound interesting. Just never heard of blue blood." She smiled… "Well, except in aristocratic people, and that doesn't count." She giggled. "Could be something of interest to me."

"Are you planning a career in science?"

"No, but I do have to write a research paper, and I have no idea about a subject." She shrugged at the thought.

"You're B. W.'s daughter, I assume."

"Yes. I'm sorry. I didn't introduce myself. I'm Persia Plemons. How rude of me."

"Nice to meet you." He looked into her eyes with a perplexed intensity. "Well, why don't I send you some material on this little animal… if that would help. We have all kinds of data, test results, environmental data and such. Be glad to if you'd like."

"Good golly, it'd save my day. I sure would appreciate it."

"Be glad to," he repeated."

"I graduate in a month, and time is short." She pulled out a pen and notepad from her purse and jotted his address on it. "This will save my day," she repeated and handed it to him.

As the evening passed, she mingled among the crowd, stopping to introduce herself and kid with one after another, joshing to witty comments regarding her good looks and their surprise that B. W. had a daughter so pretty.

"You know, B. W.'s not George Clooney," Dan Meadows, CEO

of the pipeline division, teased. "Are you sure there wasn't a mix-up somewhere along the way?"

She passed it off with a giggle but secretly wondered whether Bebe had made it known publicly that she was adopted.

The crowd scattered by ten; the business partners headed back to Hilton Head where they were to sleep, and Sherri had obviously retired to her room when Persia slipped upstairs to relax. She'd not seen Jeff depart for New Castle, and with Bebe so seemingly involved with Sherri, she decided there'd be no time alone with him either. The hurrah of the evening had ended; why not call it a day?

Inside the room, she changed into her robe and turned down the covers, deep in thought concerning the trip home the next day and thrilled that she finally had a topic for her research paper. *The Horseshow Crab.* But condensing all that data into two thousand words seemed more than formidable! She suddenly flinched at the sound of a tap on the door. Gracie had forgotten something, she mused, and stepped to answer.

"Baby, come join me on the porch." It was B. W. "Haven't seen much of you lately. Let me give you a hug. I'm so glad you're okay—that Jamaica trip."

"Where's Sherri?" Persia asked abruptly.

"She played eighteen holes of golf today. She's tired."

"Oh."

"What did you think of her? Quite pretty, don't you think?"

"Not anything like Mumsy… nothing at all. Are you gonna marry her, Bebe? It's so soon."

"She's just a friend. I met her at the club one afternoon, and we were surprised to discover that we lived in the same condo complex."

"So now you see her regularly?"

"My back has bothered me a lot this spring, baby, and companionship helps to take my mind off it. Does that sound reasonable?" He reached for his daughter's hand.

"But Mumsy…"

"I guess it is too soon, but Claire would want me to have a life without her."

"But what about me? Mumsy's gone, and if you marry her, I won't have anyone. I don't want another mother; I've had a lot of so-called mothers already." She paused and said, "By the way, tell me about my adoption. Where did you and Mumsy find me? You've never told me."

"First, Persia (he seldom referred to her name), you will always be my little girl. Do you understand? When we found you, our lives took on new meaning; it meant the world to us. We had something to live for, and Claire was beside herself."

"But she never discussed it. What was so secret about it?"

"Claire could never have children and wanted them more than anything… even went to Russia and Romania in the hope that she could adopt a child. Not long after that, we heard from DHS in Oklahoma City that they had a little girl on their waiting list. That was you." He squeezed her hand. "And you were a doll. We were ecstatic." He leaned over and kissed her cheek.

"Jessie Hartsong, or so they told us. You were twelve at the time and pretty as a picture… long blond hair that lay in curls, big blue eyes."

"How did I get to be Persia?"

"Claire's idea. She loved the country over there—Middle East, and insisted on the name, thought it unusual. You remember how she liked to be different."

"Did I put up a fuss?" Suddenly, everything inside her froze like a Siberian tundra... "That she would suddenly change my name? Why couldn't I just be Jessie?"

"Honey, you were so happy to have a real home and parents, I think you would've jumped over the moon if asked to."

"What else did those people in Oklahoma City say about me?"

"That's all. I don't think they like to give out a lot of information unless for some special reason."

"But why can't it just be me and you, Bebe? I don't know Sherri... in fact, she's not very friendly to me. Everything seems different."

"How can you make such a judgment? You've only seen her once."

"Sometimes that's enough. How do you know that she's not after your money? I'm eighteen now and will graduate in a month. I can head back to Oklahoma if I want to."

"What brought that up?"

"I do have an appointment with Dr. Brody... my six-month check-up."

"Oh, yes. Are you feeling okay?" He got up to leave. "I hope you get a good report."

Later, sprawled across the bed, she repeated the name—Jessie Hartsong. That was her real name. But did I have brothers and sisters? Who were my parents? Suddenly, the fog returned. Everything was a blur that eased her off to sleep.

Chapter 15

While spring slipped away in California, Joe gained an inch—4'11" now. Gained a pound, too, 103… all due to Claudia's good food. She'd insisted he eat at the table; those pork chops, steaks, and veggies sure tasted good after a workout with the horses! Claudia was good like that, caring and warm. Joe took to her like a chick to a mother hen!

Sometimes, Chub joined them for a meal; at which time, the conversation always ran to horses, which Joe didn't mind. He got a kick out of tales of her trainer's former days at tracks pretty much all over and how he'd gained status as a trainer. Joe listened intently in order to absorb every ounce of knowledge that Chub put out.

Spring brought other changes, too. Joe rode the mustang every chance he got, always thinking of his first horse, Rusty, back in Oklahoma. In another way, it boosted his ego to demonstrate his skills before Roslynn, who watched from the corral gate, dying to have her own chance at riding. He'd allowed her on Rascal a few times, he leading the horse while she sat in the saddle, which wasn't to her liking at all; she wanted full control. He'd merely frown at her pleadings, scoff mildly, and go through with the original plan. The colt wasn't ready for someone so inexperienced, he'd tell her and caution her to wait. She'd frown, drop her head, and run back to the gate to sit atop it to watch. For her to attempt to ride too soon, he'd say, could get dangerous.

As time passed, Chub relinquished not only all the grooming duties but the exercise workouts to Joe, which meant he breezed and galloped the thoroughbreds on a regular basis. By doing so, he learned their habits, sensitivities, and running abilities. Finally, something had opened to him. Even the drudgery of mucking stables didn't seem half as bad if he got the chance to ride the colts on a sunny day. His knowledge of horses was growing, too... all the little details; when to nudge them, to prod them, how to sense their reflexes, and how to—as Chub admonished—get the horse to perform on its own. "It's all in the hands," Chub would say. "Communicate with your hands. The horse will sense your touch." Sure enough, Chub was right. Joe practiced every aspect of it and found the advice right on target. Even Chub's early moods at times didn't deter Joe's hunger for knowledge... horses had filled a void for him since childhood. As he matured, the passion grew.

Spring days found him busy with the thoroughbreds, mostly Blazzy Star and High Pockets, but if he took a hankering to gallop the palomino, he'd put the saddle on the filly and spin off down the trail.

It was the thoroughbreds, though, that got his attention. Sometimes, he galloped them four furlongs, then five and later six, sometimes setting a stop watch to time the run, always eager to see their racing speed. Were they balkers that held back at first, then plunged forward to finish toward the end, or front runners, eager to run from the very onset? Day after day, he studied the colts' behavior, sometimes making a change under the wise advice of Chub. Later, too, when the spring meets around the country began, he watched races on TV in order to study the big-stakes colts and the jockeys that rode them, observing their tactics like a science.

"I think we'd do well to make a claimer out of Blazzy Star," Chub said to Joe one morning in mid-April. "The colt shows promise, but Claudia has her heart set on High Pockets. She thinks he'll be the one to go for the big time… high stakes."

Joe looked at him, puzzled. "She does? But Star can run."

"High Pockets does have the better pedigree. Has some mighty good blood in his veins. She might be right." Chub had a habit of turning his head to the side when he spoke.

"But don't claimers have to run first? Win a race?"

Just run or, yeah, enter a race." Chub rubbed his brow. "That's what I meant. We'd take him to the track and see what he will do. Wanna go?"

Joe, stunned at Chub's invitation, thought his luck had come. "Where?"

"Over at Arcadia… Santa Anita Track. They have races Wednesday through Sunday during their spring meet." Chub had never talked to him man-to-man. "Well, this is Tuesday. Why not tomorrow? They'll be open. Ever been to a big racetrack?"

"Can't say that I have. Where is Arcadia?"

"Not far outta Pasadena. Some nice areas over there. A theme park not far from it, too." It's one of the largest racing facilities in this country," Chub explained.

"Tomorrow, you say?"

"Yeah, you need to learn how it's done. That is, if you ever plan to get into the irons yourself."

"Ride, you mean? I ride every day."

"No, become a jockey. You definitely have the size for it."

Joe proudly lifted his shoulders. "Sure take a lot of push and shove to get anywhere in it."

"But look, son. Anything you do in life that's worthwhile takes dedication, work."

"Guess so. So we're to take Star to the track tomorrow?

"Think so, and then put every ounce of energy into High Pockets. Make sure that colt goes all the way to the top." Chub gave him a confident nod and a determined grin.

* * * *   * * * *   * * * *

At the track the next day, Joe had mixed emotions as he watched Chub coax Star from the trailer into a stable. Chub's insistence that he accompany him to the track gave him enormous pride; finally, the trainer was treating him as a man.... A business partner of sorts. It sure lifted his spirits, yet the idea of losing another good horse weighed on his heart something awful. He'd worked with Star for months and to break the relationship wasn't easy. But Chub was in charge, knew best, he kept telling himself as he pitched a handful of hay to Star and offered water one last time. As usual, Star lifted his upper lip and nuzzled his hand in appreciation. Joe brushed the colt's nose with his hand... something he'd done so many times before. As the claimer procedure came to mind, he realized Star was to be sold. Some prospective buyer most probably would inspect the horse, place a monetary value, then watch as the race proceeded. If owners are anxious to sell, then the highest check gets the horse, and there was no reason that Star's case would be anything different. Though heartbreaking, it was a fact of the business, Joe told himself as he glanced up to see Mel Sturgess, a jockey, appear in his bright silks ready for the race. Mel soon began to question Chub as to racing techniques to apply. Joe listened to Chub detail how to get the most from Star. "Let him start quick and settle into his own stride," Chub said. "Ask more of 'im on the last stretch. I think he'll respond."

Joe listened and watched Mel, curious as to how he and the colt would get along, a little jealous as to why he wasn't the one to race Star. He'd worked with the colt the longest. He'd keep his opinions to himself. No point in making waves when life was going so well.

Chub gave Mel last minute instructions before the paddock judge called, "Rides up," and in minutes the bell rang and the gates opened. Joe watched anxiously as Mel and Star got off. More than once, he cringed when Mel failed to spur the colt forward, push him a little harder. Star could do it. "Demand it of 'im," Joe shouted when Star fell behind by a length and anticipation mounted toward the finish. "Damn," Chub shouted, disappointed that Mel brought the colt in at 59.03, a loss of a length. Joe knew he could have done better, but in the racing business, there would always be winners and losers, he told himself. He'd keep silent and let Chub handle it in his way.

Afterwards, Joe was surprised when Chub held up a twenty-grand check. Star had a buyer; exactly what Chub wanted! And it showed; his face beamed like a new moon. Joe, somewhat sad, pretended to share the trainer's elation, but Star was gone—gone out into the racing world beyond!

Driving back to the ranch, Joe said to Chub, "I hate to see that colt go. Do you think we should have kept Star?"

"It's hard to say. It's hard to predict horses. Sometimes the best pedigree don't insure the best results. It helps. That's about the size of it."

"Probably," Joe commented, his mind still full of Star.

"It's always safer to bid on a good bloodline or have an agent to. You take, for example, High Pockets. He comes with very good credentials. I believe the colt will do wonders."

"He runs good for me," Joe murmured. "I have faith in 'im."

Back at the ranch, Chub let Joe out before he pulled the pickup with the trailer hitched behind down beside the barn for the night. As always, he would make sure all compartments of the stables were locked down and secure. What thief wouldn't like to get his hands on a prize animal like High Pockets?

Inside, Joe ran to tell Claudia the news—that Star had brought a good price, but to his astonishment, she was nowhere around. Both cars were in the garage and everything was in place. Surely she was around someplace. Or had she gone to a movie or shopping with a friend? he mused as a taxi pulled into the driveway and let her out. Her ordinarily perfectly made-up face was flushed and her hair flew in all directions. Never had he seen her eyes, usually bright and clear, so puffy and red.

"No. I'm not all right. I'm worried crazy. That damned mustang threw Roslynn an hour or so ago and pawed her terribly. She's seriously injured."

"She is? Oh, my." Joe stood agog, his muscles taut, his gut knotted.

"You didn't warn her," Claudia erupted, her voice cracking sporadically.

"But I did. I warned her to stay off him. That he wasn't ready for her. He's just now allowing me to saddle 'im up."

Claudia glared at him. "But you knew she was eager to ride and—" Her voice cracked again. "You left that colt in the corral where she had access. Why didn't you put him out to pasture? She'd never have caught him out there."

"I had my mind on Blazzy Star, I guess. I wouldn't have had this happen for the world, Claudia. You know how I cared for Roslynn."

"Well, look, apologies sometimes come too late. Go gather your belongings, Joe, and leave. You're fired."

"Leave? But ma'am"—It'd been months since he'd referred to her as ma'am—"I've never told you this, but I don't have a home, nowhere to go. Haven't had since I was five, just foster homes. That's the reason I found your place. A foster dad of mine just up and sold my horse, Rusty. Thought I was spending too much time with 'im. I ran away, and luckily I found your place. Please let me stay. I like it here," he pleaded.

Claudia didn't flinch. "Well, young man, I can't be concerned with your past. My godchild is lying up there in the St. Andrew's Hospital with back injuries. She may not survive, may never walk again. Both you and that crazy mustang have to go. I'm calling Al Stanford in a few minutes to come and pick him up."

"But Roslynn loves her horse. Just a few more weeks, and he'd do fine with her. Are you sure—"

"I'll give her the palomino if she recovers."

Joe glanced down, not wanting her to see the tears in his eyes. The day at the track was perfect. Now all this! "But I'm happy here. I like horses. Please, ma'am, won't you reconsider?"

"No," Claudia blurted out, still red-faced. "I want you off my premises, Joe. I can't trust your judgment anymore." She opened her purse. "Here's five one-hundred dollar bills to help you on your way."

Broken in spirit, Joe took the money, folded it and stuck it deep into his pocket. Turning toward the tack shop, he hurried to gather his few things before Chub came from the barn. It was getting dark, and the two-mile stretch to Miss Lily's where he'd spend the night was before him. Everything had happened too fast. He didn't even have the chance to share Star's success with Claudia... no use now. Whispering Trails was history. Where'd he'd go, he had no idea. He'd sleep on it and set out at dawn the next morning. Nothing really mattered—well, except horses. He wanted to ride horses, work 'em, and care for 'em. They were the only family he had.

CHAPTER 16

SAD AND IRRITATED, JOE ambled toward the gate to the main road. His backpack that contained a few of his most cherished items weighed heavy on his young shoulders as he trudged along in no mood to leave Claudia's ranch, the best home he'd found since the Murphy's back in Oklahoma. The memory of Claudia's angry, red face brought chills; she'd never chewed him out before. It just wasn't like her. Why, he wondered, did he leave Roslynn's mustang in the corral? How stupid of me, he muttered, as he regretfully recounted the incident. Roslynn always listened to me from the first day her colt arrived. To think she's now in the hospital from injuries that Claudia thinks I caused. Guess I just got carried away with the chance to go to the track with Chub... all the attention he gave me. Well, and the sale of Blazzy Star wasn't easy, either. I loved that horse, he recounted.

Golly, what if Roslynn died? He needed to go see her. It was the least he could do, and it might impress Claudia. Make her change her mind about letting him go. But to St. Andrew's? How? He didn't drive; owned no car even if he did.

Twilight gave way to dusk; only oncoming traffic lit the road enough for him to make his way back to Miss Lily's. Suddenly, a thought surfaced. Why not ask her to drive him to St. Andrew's? He inhaled deeply as if relieving stress. On second thought, did the old woman still drive? She must have seen her seventy-fifth birthday. She owned a car all right, but ask her to drive ten miles after dark? Not a good idea. Might cause another accident. Besides, he didn't know Miss Lily that well—avoided her like crazy. Sometimes, older widows ask too many questions such as, "Why aren't you with your family?" or "Why aren't you in school?" No, not a good idea, he convinced himself and stuck his hand down into his pocket to feel the crisp one-hundred dollar bills that Claudia gave him; his only security, he told himself as he sauntered along, stepping to the narrow shoulder of the road with the approach of each oncoming vehicle. When a taxi whizzed by, he adjusted his backpack and looked around. Miss Lily's place wasn't far; he'd get rid of his load. Again, he stuck his hand into his pocket and felt the cash… more money than he'd had in some time. A cab? Why not use some of it and hitch a cab to go see Roslynn? The ten-mile trip might cost him fifty or more, especially if he asked the driver to wait while he ran up, but if it'd ease his conscience, it'd be worth it, and by chance Claudia might have cooled off—be willing to forgive and take him back. It was worth a try.

Lights shone more brightly now. At the sight of the local McDonald's, his hunger got to him. A juicy burger with plenty of fries, he thought. Yep, he was hungry. A visit to the hospital could wait!

Inside, he stepped in line to order at the counter where a boisterous high school crowd clamored to place their orders, then dashed to find seats with their friends. Joe ordered, paid the cashier, and glanced about for a booth or table… every place was taken except one far back next to the door. He hurried to claim it.

"Can we join ya?" a perky blond asked when she and her friend, a redhead, approached. She set her tray on the table.

"Sure, have a seat," Joe greeted, happy to have company.

The redhead pushed in beside her friend and blurted, "I'm Kristi. What's your name?" She stared at Joe with big, brown eyes.

"Joe, Joe Hartsong." He unfolded his napkin.

"She's Mandy," the redhead said, gesturing toward her friend.

"That's me," Mandy mumbled. "You go to Carterville High?"

"No, a private school." For a moment he couldn't think of a private school, then muttered, "Parkland," a name he'd heard on TV. "But mostly I'm a horse whisperer."

"A what?" Kristi asked with a blank stare. "Is that like a jockey?"

"Yeah, sorta. I ride and gallop horses—train mustangs, too."

"Where?" Mandy inquired, looking surprised.

"Whispering Trails mostly." He scooted slightly, afraid the girls might smell his sweaty body odor. The day at the track with Chub had left no time for a shower. His tawny hair felt greasy and his jeans showed two days' grime.

"Ever get bucked?" Mandy asked as she motioned for the ketchup.

"Nope. That's beginner's stuff," he bragged, glad to show the girls his talent. He picked up a fry and choked it down. "In fact, I have a friend in the hospital right now who got bucked off today—pretty serious injuries, she got, too."

"Her horse bucked her, you say? Why? Did something scare 'im?"

"No, it's a mustang I've been training. She got on 'im before he was ready—saddle broke. Didn't listen to me when I cautioned her against it."

"Really?" Kristi said.

"She slipped into the corral while I was away." Suddenly, he remembered Claudia's outburst.

"How old is she?" Kristi continued to inquire.

"Thirteen." The taste of his burger seemed to relieve some of the tension. First food he'd had since breakfast. Chub didn't take time for lunch at noon.

"Is she gonna be all right—okay?" Mandy asked.

"Gosh, I sure hope so." Joe shook his head. "Sure sorry it happened." He glanced away as he remembered Roslynn, the cute girl with the big eyes and laughing face. "I sure would like to see her, but my car broke down." He glanced away, feeling guilty for the lie.

"You old enough to drive?" Kristi asked, obviously surprised. For a moment she stared at him as if in disbelief.

"Have a permit, fifteen."

"I thought you were about twelve or thirteen," Kristi confessed. "Guess jockeys do have to be small. You ride in big races?"

"Not real big—not yet, not until I'm sixteen at least, but yeah, I gallop and race, race a lot." He realized he'd stretched the truth somewhat. It got easier with time. Actually, he'd never entertained the idea of becoming a jockey, except Chub mentioned it once.

"You sure have the body for it," Mandy commented and wiped her lips with her napkin.

He glared at her, feeling self-conscious. Did he really look twelve?

"Guess so," he muttered, finishing his food. "Guess I'll hail a cab if I go see my friend." He stood. "Nice to meecha," he said, about to leave.

"Look, if you need a ride we can take you. Can't we, Kristi?" Mandy glanced toward her friend for an answer.

"Yeah, sure. St. Andrew's, you say? Not that far, is it?"

"I sure will appreciate it. I kinda blame myself for the accident." He sat down again while the girls finished their food. "I sure hate that it happened."

"Look," Kristi began. "If I's you, I'd not worry. That little gal didn't follow the rules. If she gets well, she oughta have her buns spanked, if you ask me."

Joe didn't comment. "Are ya'll sure you don't mind?"

"Don't mind a bit. Nothing else to do. Well, I do have a math test to study for, but I hate math. Sure we'll take ya," Kristi continued.

"I just live up the street." He pointed. "Mind if I run home for a quick shower? I've spent the day at the racetrack."

"Not if you hurry." Mandy again glanced at her friend as if to check with her.

"Be back in twenty minutes," Joe said and got up to go. "Can I meet you here?"

"Sure, we'll wait."

Outside, he sprinted across the parking lot, his backpack flopping against his shoulders. When car lights flashed, he looked at his watch—7:45. A dash to his room at Miss Lily's to freshen up should take less than fifteen minutes, to get back to the girls by 8:15. Elated, he smiled that for once luck had come his way. A visit with Roslynn in the hospital seemed the decent thing to do, and by chance, Claudia might notice, too. No way he could lose.

Oops, his foot suddenly slipped—loose gravel! His rear hit the pavement with a plop, and his backpack flew open with everything strewn in all directions—photos, books, and his best pair of sneakers! Scurrying in the darkness, he raked his hand over the pavement to recover them, frantic that some of his most prized possessions were lost in the night!

Finally at his room at Miss Lily's, he stripped nude, jumped in the shower, and thoroughly soaped his body. The warm water felt relaxing, and the hope that he quite possibly might have another chance with Claudia buoyed his spirits. "Those crazy gals thought I was a jockey," he mumbled as water flowed over his face. "A jockey of all things. How did a fella ever manage to ride those big boys... thoroughbreds... at the track? He reapplied shampoo to his hair, still pondering the jockey idea. Too much to think of now, them girls are waitin'. Better hurry. He jumped out of the shower and dried off, happy that hopes of turning his disappointment with Claudia around.

He dressed and headed back to McDonald's. Inside he glanced around for the girls—Kristy and Mandy, but to his chagrin saw nothing of them. "Guess they gave up on me," he mumbled, disappointed and angry. Then he headed back to Mss Lily's for the night.

CHAPTER 17

Back at Miss Lilly's, Joe lay in his narrow bed, tired and depressed, his hands behind his head that throbbed as if a hammer hit it. Claudia's outburst that hit like a fist between the eyes was still fresh on his mind. Why did she blame him for Roslynn's accident? He'd warned the girl repeatedly not to get on the mustang. The colt was only partially saddle-broken, but what good did it do to dwell on it? Claudia expressed herself quite clearly. He was flat-out fired with orders to leave and not come back! He stared at the single light bulb that dangled from the ceiling with a dusty spider web attached to it. What were his options? Come morning, he'd leave—leave his key on the dresser with a ten-dollar bill and slip out without a word with Miss Lily. She'd soon realize that he'd gone; that was good enough. The less said the better. Suddenly, the headache worsened, and he felt a nauseated feeling coming on. What on earth would he do if he got sick?

At dawn the next morning, as planned, he gathered his few

belongings—an extra pair of jeans, some photos of Roslynn's mustang Rascal, and a small booklet he'd picked up at the racetrack, and set out toward the main road. If luck smiled, he'd hitch a ride to Interstate 40, which ran across country, and from there one direction seemed as good as another. He'd seen the West already; the East struck him as interesting. Both New York and Florida offered racing facilities. Kentucky raised great horses, and Oaklawn in Arkansas got big winners. The trip to Santa Anita with Chub cinched his desire to race—ride the big winners, but the odds against a runaway teen with no credentials or funds offered little assurance of success. He'd not mull that now. Even the rosy hues of sunrise somehow perked his spirits. Out on the main road, he stuck up his thumb as a pickup truck approached, and he gasped with glee when it stopped!

"Where ya headin', young man?" the friendly-faced driver said.

"Toward Interstate 40, sir." Again, he used his best manners.

"That's some distance away. Where ya headed?" the driver repeated.

Joe hesitated. "Headin' east, I guess, uh, yes sir, east it is." Confused and tired from the lack of sleep, he didn't care to expand. How did he know where he was headed?

The driver glanced at him strangely. "School's out for summer already?"

"Yes, sir." Again, he didn't elaborate. Who felt like talking so early in the morning?

The driver let him out at the interstate, and it was mid-afternoon before luck prevailed again… a semi eased up to offer a ride.

"Where you going, young man?" the driver, probably in his sixties, asked with a mature manner about him.

"Headin' east," Joe replied in his lackadaisical manner, still depressed from thoughts of Claudia's outburst. "Guess I'll find work somewhere if I'm lucky."

"For the summer, you mean?"

"Yes, sir." Again, Joe avoided any semblance of details. Any of the major cities along Interstate 40 held promise in one way or another, but did they have racetracks? "Ever heard of Carletta Downs?" he asked the driver as they drove along.

"In New Mexico, you mean? Yeah, sure."

"Thought I might go see it." Joe raked his wet, sweaty hair to the side, fully aware that he'd seen only a few races at the track on TV. "You going into Albuquerque?"

"Gallup," the driver replied and brought mention of the grocery firm to which he was to deliver.

Joe listened, not really caring one way or the other, at times nodding off or deeply absorbed in memories of Whispering Trails.

The jaunt into Gallup went well, and at the last ramp off Interstate 40, he jumped from the truck cab and thanked the driver. Eager to move on, he ambled toward an intersection where he encountered an Native American jeweler and soon purchased a silver and turquoise ring for $50 of Claudia's money. Turquoise went well with leather boots, he decided, proudly admiring the way it enhanced his middle finger. As he loitered beside the highway, he'd occasionally stick up his thumb when an oncoming semi heading east approached.

In Albuquerque, the story was much the same. Carletta Downs, a salesman told him, was a good distance south, which if he really sought employment, might take at least a week, at which Joe shook his head.

Not like Claudia's place, he thought as the yen to visit the track faded. When a pickup truck en route to Amarillo offered a lift at a nearby truck stop, Joe gladly accepted.

"Sure, get in," the driver said after he'd filled his gas tank. "You have relatives in Amarillo?"

"Nawh. Returnin' from California. On my way to Oklahoma," Joe murmured, still confused as to where he'd end up. If the notion hit him, he might just drop in on the Murphy's. They'd sure be surprised to see him. Well, and he'd be glad to see them... sorta, still not sure as to his foster dad's motives in selling his horse. Was it love? Joe scratched his head. Love? No kind of love he wanted. No, he'd not stop in Oklahoma, he reasoned as a pickup bearing a Kentucky license plate and pulling a horse trailer passed.

"You're mighty quiet, young man. Bet you're sleepy."

"Yes, sir. Wonder what kind of horses that man is hauling. Can you see?"

"Can't tell. You like horses, I take it?"

"Yeah, sure do."

At the edge of Amarillo, before the driver was to turn north, Joe grunted a boyish "thanks" and jumped from his comfortable seat in the big truck. Spotting a pizza place, he made a dive for it and got in line next to a teen about his own age who grinned sheepishly and introduced himself as Willie. "What's yours?" he muttered and raked his scruffy hair out of his face that showed a few whiskers and a bad case of acne.

"Joe."

"Where you from?" Willie asked as he approached the counter to order.

"California. Worked on a ranch out there." Joe reached into his pocket for cash. Thanks to Claudia, he had money for food. Claudia—one nice lady, he thought with the same fondness he couldn't forget.

"California, you say? What'd you do on the ranch?"

"Galloped horses, mostly. Thoroughbreds." Joe straightened his shoulders proudly and stepped up to order a medium pepperoni.

"Come join me," Willie said, waiting for Joe to get his order.

Joe pulled out a one-hundred dollar bill. "Ain't got no change," he told the cashier and handed her the bill.

"Nothing smaller than this?" she asked with a stunned stare. "Mighty big money you're carrying around."

Joe didn't answer. To stand and chat only delayed things, and he was hungrier than a mother dog with pups. The cashier soon counted the change, and Joe followed Willie to a table at the back.

"You live around here?" he asked at the table.

"Yeah, out from here a piece," Willie answered and picked up a slice of pizza. He began to eat.

"You work?" Joe inquired in the hope that he might be so lucky.

"Sorta. Hang around a body shop. Will down there—that's the owner—he gives me work sometimes. Mainly, I'm interested in racing.

"Horses?"

"Nawh, cars."

"Oh." Joe's interest fell. "I'm interested in horse racing. Ever been to the track?"

For several minutes, they compared life experiences, at times one trying to outdo the other with a tale. Willie's life in some ways resembled his own, a lot of street experiences mostly, Joe decided, and immediately perked at the presence of a new friend.

"Like to dance?" Willie asked when they'd finished the meal and idled outside.

"Dance? Whatcha mean?"

"Two-step or line dance. Mostly Western stuff out here."

"Never tried it. Do you?"

"I go to the Horse Stall occasionally. No problem to meet girls out there. Like girls?"

"Yeah." The name of the place sure got his attention. "Where is it?"

"Out east a bit. If you wanna go tonight, I'll watch for you. Anybody can go, well, anybody over sixteen."

"I'm fifteen. Reckon I can fake it?"

"Probably. They don't check I.D.'s. Look," Willie added, "go five blocks east and you'll see a big red building—like a barn with a parking lot behind it. I'll meecha there at seven. Okay?" Willie's stare denoted insistence.

"If I'm not there by straight up seven, don't wait—never been dancin' in my life."

"Don't worry. You'll meet plenty of girls that'll teach you," Willie said before he brisked away.

"Dancin', my gosh," Joe muttered after Willie left. "Horse Stall." Sure, he'd go to see the place if nothing else... have a little fun, too. Yeah, sure, he'd meet Willie, meet 'im at seven.

That evening, Joe in his one and only outfit, jeans, T-shirt, and boots, entered the Horse Stall with backpack secured to his shoulders. To say that he felt self-conscious put it mildly. Was there a check-in window where he could leave the darn thing? On second thought, the cash that Claudia gave him was in its side pocket. No, somebody might take it. No way he'd risk it.

"Hi," he greeted Willie when he spotted Willie near the door. The band, dressed in Western wear, broke into a swing number, and several couples got up to dance. The place did have atmosphere—old plows, horse collars, and shelves of old photos adorned the ceiling and rafters. "Some place this is," Joe said when Willie directed him to a table on the west side of the dance floor.

"Do you drink?" Willie asked after they were seated.

"Nothing to speak of. They might git me, ask my age."

"Look, you got any money?" Willie asked a few minutes later. "Why don't I order and we'll share it. That way nobody'll ever know."

Joe took off his backpack, unzipped a side pocket, and took out a ten. "Here," he said. "Get what you like." Willie whizzed to the bar and Joe rezipped his backpack to wait. Yep, Willie knows the ropes all right. The evening was gonna be fun.

The beer that Willie ordered sure served as an upper. The evening passed, and more than once, he stumbled onto the dance floor with anyone who asked. The line dance was more fun than he'd ever imagined, and before he left at midnight, he'd mastered the Boot Scootin' Boogie.

But where was Willie? The scruffy-haired kid evidently left early without a single word. Probably some gal invited him home with her for the night, Joe decided, and picked up his backpack to go. With

Claudia's money, he'd not walk all the way back in to town; he'd get a motel closer and settle in for the night.

At the Easy Comfort a few minutes later, he entered and requested a room. When the desk clerk assigned him, he quickly unzipped his backpack for cash to pay. Suddenly, his heart stopped. No cash. Where was his money? Stunned and embarrassed, he mumbled, "My money's gone. Somebody must've got it."

The clerk stared with a puzzled look.

"Somebody had to've got it. I went dancin' at the Horse Stall and had it with me. Now, it's gone."

Still, the clerk waited and stared.

"I know they did... somebody-"

The clerk stepped to the side to help another guest. Joe, dumbfounded and annoyed, zipped his backpack and slung it over his shoulder to leave. "Willie, that kid at the pizza place. He saw my hundred-dollar bill and cooked the Horse Stall thing up. Well, I can't prove it," Joe told himself. "And I sure can't find the son of a gun. But me, like a dumb ass took it all in."

Outside, Joe ambled toward town for another night on the street, more anxious than ever to get on his way east with one asset to his name—the turquoise ring that he bought from the Indian in New Mexico. If he could hock it, or better still, sell it, he could eat until he reached Kentucky.

CHAPTER 18

PERSIA SQUIRMED IN THE doctor's office. What might Dr. Brody say? She felt well, had passed her schoolwork and graduated—with honors! But not without a lot of hard work; Mr. Elgard's workload gave her hives at times, especially that crazy research paper. Luckily, Reid Morgan had saved the day! He'd sent tons of data, photos, even invited her down to Charleston to see his lab. "One nice guy," she told Mr. Elgard. "I may actually take him up on it one day, but not until I have my check-up in Oklahoma." Needless to say, schoolwork came easily—but the memory lapse? Childhood memories still seemed a total gap. Those, she told herself, might never come back in any kind of detail... nothing except, as Bebe told her—her biological name, Jessie Hartsong. Not even it seemed natural anymore.

"Where ya from?" the blond-haired kid next to her asked as they waited to see the doctor. He grinned so that his eyes beamed with a youthful grin.

"Pittsburgh," Persia replied. "I'm Persia Plemons. I live in the Shadyside area there."

"Pittsburgh, Oklahoma?"

"Pennsylvania. I didn't know there was a Pittsburgh, Oklahoma." She looked at him, surprised.

"Can't prove it by me. I'm Billy Stipes."

"Nice to meecha, Billy. Did you break your leg?" She noticed the cast he wore.

"Yeah, a darn wreck. Sure won't drive so fast next time." Shook his head. "Went too fast on that crazy turnpike."

"Which one is that?"

"H. E. Bailey that goes down to Lawton."

"You're from Lawton? I think I've been to Lawton." She thought for a moment. "Know anyone there?" She hesitated. "Know anyone by the name of *Hartsong*?" It was a wild guess, she realized, but the kid might just know her mother and whether she was alive or not. She faintly remembered something of her mother's auburn hair, and the *Lawton* came to mind.

"Can't say that I do. Actually, I grew up in Kansas."

"Oh," Persia mumbled just as the nurse called Billy in to see the doctor. *Lawton*. The name resonated. The door to the waiting room opened again and the nurse called her.

"Miss Plemons," Dr. Brody greeted when he entered the examining room. "So nice to see you. How have you felt? Any headaches?"

"Not much, just occasionally, before a test." She smiled. She had forgotten how handsome he was. His gorgeous eyes danced romantically as he spoke.

"Let's take a look at your head wound. Any soreness?" He pulled her hair back. "Can't see but little scar. It has healed well. Any memory lapses? Any trouble at school?"

"I finished high school—no learning problems." She hesitated. "Just early stuff. I can't remember much about my early years."

He stood watching her as though in deep thought. "That'll probably change."

"But I was adopted. That I know. The Plemonses adopted me when I was twelve, and anything before that is a mere blur." She grimaced. "Crazy. It sounds crazy, I know."

"You'd like to connect all that, I'm sure." He smiled.

His pleasant manner put her at ease. "I guess it's just natural to want to know our ancestry."

"These cases do take time, and you know what, Miss Plemons? It *will* clear up in time. Your head wound was small. You did get a small clot, but we got to it rapidly. Fortunately, you weren't far from the hospital and care was given quickly."

"Think so?" She stared at him with question. "You're sure?"

"Let's stay optimistic. You're ahead of the game—planning for college, I guess."

"Yes." Her eyes met his with concern.

"Let's see what another six months brings. I'll want to see you then." He patted her arm. "And don't react too jubilantly if you are suddenly able to remember everything as clear as crystal." He laughed. "Our brains do unusual feats."

"I hope you're right," she said, totally fascinated by his friendly disposition and good looks. She thanked him and smiled on her way out.

With the appointment behind her, she hurried to her hotel to change clothes. The mention of H. E. Bailey Turnpike and Lawton resurfaced. Billy Stipes mentioned Lawton, but how did one get to Lawton? He mentioned that the turnpike went south to Lawton. Why did the mere mention of the place hit her so plainly? It stuck in her mind like a postage stamp.

The sun shone through the windshield of the car she'd rented; the June morning was nice. But where or how did one get onto a turnpike that headed toward Lawton?

A few minutes later, as expected, the clerk instructed her to turn onto Highway 44 West and intersect with Interstate 40 that would lead to H. E. Bailey Turnpike. The day appeared to promise an easy drive south; she was game. The trip might result in nothing, but what did she have to lose?

A few miles south, the road curved and twisted along red dirt fields, cottonwood trees, and windmills. Windmills! she exclaimed. I remember that I watched them spin in the wind when we'd travel to the city! And the rolling grasslands, velvety lush with patches of wild flowers! Canyons, too. We had canyons around Carlisle. Carlisle! That's where we lived... ten miles north of Lawton! Sure did! My mother worked at a bar in Lawton, and Joe Dee and I stayed at home—well, except when I occasionally got to ride the school bus to go to school. *Hartsong*—that was our name. My dad fell from a scaffold and died. It's all clear now. My gosh, it is. I'll have to tell Dr. Brody! But I won't get to see him again for six months. Six months! I could look at that handsome man every day. Six months, darn! A road sign read *Chickasha* and she continued south. My word, I can't believe this! It's just too surreal.

At a Lawton sign, she turned right and pulled into a service station.

Inside, a young attendant smiled and stepped forward. "May I help you?" he asked. His hair was windblowm and his face greasy.

"My name is Persia Plemons." She noticed he appeared quite young. "I've lived away for awhile and am looking for my relatives by the name of *Hartsong*. Do you know anyone by that name?"

"Hartsong?" He thought for a moment. "Hartsong," he repeated. "Can't say that I do. Here in Lawton, you mean?"

"Well, Carlisle, mainly… this general area."

"You might wanna ask somebody older is all I could suggest."

Downtown, she pulled into the library parking lot to go inside. Two middle-age-appearing women sat behind a wide checkout desk and watched as she approached.

"Hi," she began in a polite manner. "Have either of you lived here long?"

One stared questioningly; the other replied, "All my life. How can I help you?"

"Would you happen to know anyone by the name of Hartsong? I have relatives by that name, and I've lost touch. They used to live here—well at Carlisle mostly." A dart-like pang struck her deeply… how long it had been since she left the little town. Something about it all felt odd—strange! Tears misted her eyes. She subtly wiped them away and said, "I'd really like to find them."

"I remember," one of the women began, "when Wesco Oil built their plant up at Anadarko, that a Hartsong man fell to his death, but that's too long ago, I guess. I didn't know him, anyway."

"Did you know his wife?" Persia asked. "Or his family?"

"No, just heard it on the news. Never knew him at all." The woman turned toward the other woman. "Would you know, Elsie?"

"Too early for me. We moved here from North Carolina three years ago. I'm no help."

"So that's the only Hartsong you've known?" Persia asked, disappointed.

"'Fraid so. Sorry, hon, that I can't help more. You say your name is *Plemons?*" The woman's expression brightened.

"Yes'm."

"Would you be related to the Plemons at Wesco Oil? We're accustomed to hearing of them. They donate a lot of money to projects here."

"Yes, ma'am. I'm his daughter," she replied barely above a whisper. "B. W. Plemons is my dad."

"His daughter?" one woman said with a gasp.

"Well, bless your heart, honey. So glad you dropped in. We're so glad to meet ya."

"Thanks," Persia said and turned to go. As she walked toward the door, she overheard one woman say to the other, "What do you think about her? I didn't know B. W. Plemons had a daughter or any other relatives in this area. He's from Pennsylvania." She raised an eyebrow.

"Me, neither. Do you reckon she really is his daughter?"

"Sakes alive, I don't guess the girl would lie."

Outside, Persia got into the rental car and sat thinking. Should she drive on out to Carlisle? But would it prove anything? Her mother, most likely, had died already from alcoholism. And Joe Dee? He could be anywhere. Poor little guy! How well I remember fixing his breakfast every morning. No, I'll try another day. But she would tell Bebe... tell him that her memory was normal again, hurrah! As for her real family, no hint of them anywhere... too much water under the bridge, she told herself and started the car for the trip back to the city!

CHAPTER 19

"Bebe," Persia squealed into the phone that evening. "I'm home. I had my checkup."

"How'd it go, sweetie?"

"Great... I feel like a big, juicy watermelon all sugary and ripe!" she giggled, happy to report good news. "My memory's back."

"My, you're poetic."

"I can remember everything. I'm back to normal."

"You're sure? What did the doctor say?"

"You know, it was strange. He said my memory would come back suddenly, and it did. I was driving down the highway, and it hit me like a dart. Everything about my early childhood was as clear as glass."

"You'll have to tell me." B. W.'s voice as usual sounded warm and caring. "Tell me all about your early years."

"Will you come home soon? I want to see you."

"Not right away. Sherri wants us to go to St. Petersburg and Scandinavia—Norway, mostly. I think her ancestry is there."

Stunned, Persia sat mortified… Sherri again. "And you're letting her make all the plans? She doesn't look Norwegian. Rather Spanish, I'd say."

"This is something she's had on her mind for a long time, hon. She found an article on the cruise in a travel magazine and I can't talk her out of it." He sounded apologetic.

"You're still all wrapped up in her, it seems. I'll talk to you later."

"I'm glad you're well," he mumbled the way he always did when he realized he'd irked his daughter.

"See ya," she snapped and put down the phone. "When will he ever wake up?" she mumbled. "That woman is out for his money. I know it. I know it !"

Opening her mail, she hurriedly read Reid Morgan's note. "How did the research paper go? Let me know the outcome," he'd written. She pitched it down and tore open Jeff Lorton's letter. He was to come to town the following Friday, and would she join him for dinner? Friday? She thought. Five days away! She quickly scribbled a note to the affirmative and put it in the mail. Jeff Lorton! A great antidote for Bebe's shenanigans—a cruise with Sherri Tahlwald of all things! Too angry to concentrate, she stepped to the window. Bebe just ruined my day… my recovery! I can't believe he'd behave so insensitively. After all the uncertainty, he acts so casual about it. Memories of my early childhood in Oklahoma! Joe Dee must have turned fifteen by now, as an image of the blonde kid with freckles flashed before her. And Mama? Wonder what became of her… probably dead from all the drinking. Foster kids at best experience so many turns and twists in their lives—unless, of course, they're adopted into good homes. Recently, though, with

Mumsy gone and Bebe already involved with another woman, their happy home was probably gone forever!

Jeff Horton arrived on time Saturday evening as dapper as a Wall Street banker, yet not at all reserved. He laughed a lot, kidded constantly, and knew exactly how to amuse her. Guess that's why Bebe hired him, Persia told herself as he opened the car door for her. He's definitely good with people. Just another example of Bebe's good head for business, even if he is at times obnoxious—that Tahlwald woman; how could he?

"So how's your work going?" she asked as he turned the car around to leave.

"I've signed five leases since our trip to Beaufort. Couldn't go better. And you?"

"I graduated from high school, then went to Oklahoma. Both went well." She cringed in the hope that he wouldn't ask why. The memory lapse might come across to him as eerie... strange, to say the least.

"You have relatives in Oklahoma?"

"Did, but they've moved away."

Somehow the subject was dropped as they recalled with laughter the Beaufort trip, details of the reception, and how they almost missed the route to the reception at Scarlett's Parlor.

At the Palisades, a state-of-the-art restaurant where the elite of Pittsburgh dined, Persia wondered whether her outfit was appropriate... white slacks and a red off-the-shoulders top. Too bad she no longer had Mumsy to advise her. Mumsy watched her own appearance religiously; knew exactly what to wear and where. Some classy lady she was. I miss her.

"A penny for your thoughts," Jeff whispered at a table near a window.

"Missing my mom, I guess."

"How's that?"

"She's gone—killed in a plane crash. You didn't know?"

"Guess I wasn't with Wesco then."

The waiter came and they ordered.

"Is your dad—Mr. Plemons—adjusting okay? I seldom see him."

"Guess so. He's spent most of the spring in Florida." She rolled her eyes. "Another woman."

"Florida?"

"Palm Beach. We have property there." She hesitated. "Yep, to tell the truth, I think he's met somebody already—a lady friend." She rolled her eyes again. "Remember, she accompanied him to the reception in Beaufort? She's the one. He says she's Norwegian. I think she's Spanish."

"I didn't notice. I guess I had my eyes on someone else." He reached for her hand and squeezed it.

"It's hard to grow up without parents," she whispered almost in tears. "So hard."

"Perhaps he'll give you a step-mother," Jeff said, and continued to hold her hand.

Persia jerked her hand from his. "I hope not." She wanted to say more but didn't, except to say, "I guess I have to grow up now and accept life as it is. It's just that my mother always took me to New York on a shopping spree each spring and a million other happy occasions… I really miss that, Jeff."

"I know how you feel. My mother died when I was fifteen," he reflected. "It was hard for me, as well. She always selected my outfits and made sure I shampooed my hair." He chuckled with a boyish freshness. Something about him seemed so real.

"I wondered where you got your good taste in clothes."

"Thanks. So are you gonna stay in Pittsburgh for the summer? I'd like to see more of you."

"Until fall. I'll enroll at the University here." She paused. "At least for my first two years."

As they dined, the conversation ran from school to travel—he had aspirations to travel to Europe someday—especially Austria to see the Morgans' birthplace. He'd taken piano lessons as a child and chuckled when he recalled his teacher's name—Gertie Whizenbaum. "When she chewed me out for neglecting practice, I'd secretly refer to her as *Gert.*" He laughed again with a silly smirk.

It was near ten when the meal ended. "There's a special spot I want you to see," he said as he started the car.

"Tell me," she began, "what do you do for a pastime... besides piano, that is?"

"I don't play piano much anymore. Mostly golf or tennis. Except this fall I'm starting to law school."

"And quit your job?"

"No, some evening and Saturday classes. I've found that my M.B.A. isn't enough. I write leases. Those mineral rights can get complicated at times."

"I see. As I said earlier, I'm also enrolling, but do you know for the life of me, I have no idea what I'll study. Did you know all that when you first entered college?"

"Actually, I can't remember." He laughed and turned into an overlook near the river's edge. "I want you to see this place before we drive home. You'll love it."

"How did you find this?" Awestruck, she glanced out to see the reflections of city lights as they danced and shimmered on the water's surface. A round June moon, orange and mellow, hung in the eastern sky like a Japanese woo lantern.

"Just ran into it."

"I'd say you have a good sense of discovery. You must be a romantic."

"I explore a lot. Remember, I write land leases." He laughed again.

"Only land leases?" she whispered. How many other dates had he brought to this place? "I guess I shouldn't have asked." She giggled.

He didn't comment, just reached for her hand. "I usually find what I want." He winked.

"Wish I could say the same," she mumbled, still reflecting on her early years.

"Whatta ya mean?"

"Lost a cousin once." She'd dare not say *brother*. Jeff knew nothing of her upbringing.

"Since when? I mean how long ago?"

"Almost ten years. He must be fifteen by now. I have no idea how to find a long-lost relative. Would you?" She attempted to turn it into a humorous comment.

"Aren't there agents who search for missing persons?"

"Beats me, but how long might something such as that take?"

"You'd have to ask an expert. Outta my field of knowledge." He drew her to him. "I do know one thing. I've wanted to kiss you since the Beaufort trip, and doggone it, I had to up and leave early that night."

The warmth of his arms felt comforting and real as she caught a whiff of his clean, fresh fragrance. Impulsively, she lifted her lips to his in ecstasy that literally took her breath away.

"Your nose is cold," he finally whispered. "Hot lips and cold nose." He chuckled and kissed her again.

"Guess so," she whispered as their lips met again and again in a fever of passion. "You must have scads of women after you," she said later. "You sure know how to kiss."

"I was too busy in college to date much… well, except for one, and she skipped off to Italy after graduation," he confided.

"Why Italy?"

"To go to culinary school. Wanted to learn to make gourmet foods, I guess. I dunno. You'd have to ask her. All I know is that she wanted to someday have a TV cooking show." He sighed. "Silly gal."

"She must've cooked well… had a knack for it, I guess."

"She just up and left. That's all I know." He got a far-away look for a moment.

"And left you heartbroken?" Persia sensed his indignation.

"Oh, not really." He hesitated. "Just surprised. I had no idea she'd planned it." He glanced out toward the river. "Please, let's change the subject," he retorted. "I've found better fish to fry." He winked. "I'm kinda a one gal at a time kind of guy. If you know what I mean."

"So I'm a fish?" She snuggled up to him. "Angel fish or puffer?"

"You're silly, Persia Plemons, but I like it." He lowered his lips to hers for a long lingering connection. "You make me feel young," he said later. "Let's forget about anyone else."

For a moment Persia said nothing. Petrified by his affection, she felt her heart race and her chest tighten. He was divine; wonderful! She wanted more, more. "You sound as if you're ancient," she whispered. "Early twenties, I'd guess."

"Twenty-four to be exact. I should know what I want by now," he said as they readied to go.

"Do we ever really know?" she answered on the way home. "Is love that certain?"

CHAPTER 20

"WHAT ARE YOUR PLANS for the Fourth?" Jeff asked when he called on Tuesday. He sounded more upbeat than usual.

"Not much. My dad's on a cruise, I reckon, and the housekeeper's on vacation. And you?"

"Let's go somewhere."

"A movie, you mean?"

"No, out of town for the weekend."

Surprised, she wondered what it was with him. Out of town with a man? Bebe would have a hissy-fit if he knew... her at the mercy of a male far from home. "To where? When is the Fourth, anyway—the day of the week?"

"It's next Monday, and I get Friday off as well. Thought we might spend some time at the folks' cabin."

For a minute, every function of her body froze—stopped! Had he lost his mind? "Where is this place?" She finally asked, trying to come up with a decent refusal.

"You'd love it. Listen to this, Persia. It's nested among hills with the prettiest little lake and wildflowers everywhere. Thought we might grill some steaks, and oh, yeah, do you like to hike?"

"Where is it?" she repeated.

"Upper part of Virginia, just west of Berkley Springs. Ever been there?"

"How would we get there?"

"I think we could drive in a day. I'm ready to get out of town… enjoy the wild for a change, breathe fresh air. Want to?"

With Bebe out of town and Maud away with her brother, Jeff's invitation came at just the right moment. Clairmont seemed deserted now, like a house without a family. Her dates with Jeff had been the only spark of the summer. Even casual events with Molly had lost some of their luster. Besides, Molly worked fulltime at the city library. Whether it was Bebe's involvement with Sherri or the loss of Mumsy, summer at the big house was dull, lonely, even eerie at times. A trip with Jeff struck her as exciting, different—well, why not? Jeff had convinced her that the cabin had two bedrooms, one upstairs and one down. "You can sleep in the bunk upstairs," he'd said with a chuckle!

* * * * * * * * * *

The cabin and its surroundings were everything Jeff had said, pretty, comfortable, and definitely a romantic hideaway. Why, she wondered, had he chosen the place. But she'd already decided not to analyze the situation too much. Have fun, she told herself. You're a woman now. It's time you act like one, and certainly to act like a woman with Jeff was easy; he stirred every passion in her! More than once, she'd wondered what it would be like to have him touch her, tease her uncontrollably, but then Mumsy's admonitions always resurfaced. "Act like a lady, dear. That's what men really want in a woman." But Mumsy was gone now and Bebe might as well be—always with that Sherri person. Why hadn't she seen it coming? she thought, totally disgusted! All the old stuff gone, changed! Life had to move on. From now on, she'd make her own decisions, do her own thing!

About that time, Jeff came in with the groceries... some steaks, salad greens, rolls, and potatoes. "I hope I thought of everything," he said and began to set them out. "I'll get the grill ready if you want to mix the salad."

Persia cringed. Her prepare the salad? She'd had little experience in the kitchen with Maud available to prepare meals. "I hope you don't expect too much." She glanced at him with a look of inconfidence. "I'm not that old flame of yours who flew off to Italy to study culinary science."

He stepped toward her. "Will you hush? Why ruin a nice weekend?" He brushed her cheek with a kiss and went outside to start the grill.

She washed the greens and wiped them dry with a paper towel, and as she began to cut and mix them, she occasionally glanced through the window to see him, clean-cut and sexy in shorts and T-shirt, tan as a Georgia pie crust, too. Some guy, she thought... the way he looked into her eyes made every emotion in her go bonkers!

* * * * * * * * * * * *

After the meal and a brief rest on the deck, Jeff suggested a hike. "There's a shady trail that runs along the lake," he said. "It's nice and interesting." He reached for her hand and pulled her up from the chair. "Let's go explore it."

"Any wildlife? Wildflowers?"

"Might jump a rabbit or see a squirrel… butterflies, too. Wanna go see?" He smiled at her.

Already in shorts and a tank top, she followed him to the lawn's edge where he took her hand for the stroll. A soft breeze blew through her hair, and the air smelled of wild daisies. "Any birds around here?" she asked, hoping to see some wild ducks.

"Probably. Hey, look," he shouted at the sight of a butterfly ahead. "Is that a monarch or swallowtail?"

"Swallowtails are yellow and black. That has to be a monarch. Don't you think?" Persia said and stepped closer.

"Can't prove it by me." He took her hand again. "It's pretty, though."

In the shade of a big oak tree, he stopped and, without a word, pulled her to him. Tenderly, he cupped her face in his hands and found her lips. For a breathless moment, neither spoke.

"I'm glad you're with me," he finally whispered. "I'm glad you could come."

"You don't consider me too young, Jeff? I wondered. Do I seem like a school girl?"

"Eighteen?"

"I'm nineteen."

"For me, twenty-five? No. Think of all those men who go for women twenty years their junior." He nudged her cheek with his nose. "I guess age has little to do with love. Think so?"

"If you say so." A squirrel scampered in the underbrush. "I like this place. How did your parents find it?" She was ready to change the subject.

"My mother's idea, I guess. Some realtor told her about it."

His dad? Was he alive or deceased? He never spoke of his dad.

"My dad's a salesman and travels a lot. I don't feel like I know him at times."

Persia said nothing. Every family had its problems. More than anything, she wanted to reveal her own past, open up to him, be her true self. She wanted to tell him how she was adopted by the Plemons, how she had really come from a very humble background. Jeff, she realized, only knew her as the daughter of wealthy oil people, not as a poor carpenter's daughter who had drifted in and out of foster homes for years, and a mother who seemingly cared little as to what became of her kids.

"Say," he finally asked, "did you find your cousin?"

"Cousin?"

"The one you've lost touch with. You mentioned him once."

"Oh, that. No, I guess I gave up on it." It hit her that he referred to Joe Dee. "Nope, nothing new there." Why, she told herself, go into a long sob story? She'd come to have fun, relax, forget some of the morbid details of her life. The sound of birds flitting in the branches of the tree broke the silence. "So you don't think I'm a giddy teenager?"

"Haven't you heard that love is where you find it?"

"Will you stop it? You tell me." She wrinkled her nose kiddingly.

"But it is true, Persia. Men need you women. You stabilize us, give us purpose and comfort." Again, he brushed her cheek with his nose. "I'd sure hate to think I'd spend my life alone. Wouldn't you?"

Why was he talking like this? Had he really been in love with the woman who flew off to Italy? Is he dating me on the rebound? One wonders. "You've been in love, haven't you? I mean, serious love. Tell me the truth." She stared into his eyes.

When a cardinal perched on a nearby bush, he said, "Look, there's your bird. I thought we'd see some. Have you ever seen such color?"

Not knowing how to answer, she muttered, "We have lots of birds at Clairmont." She noticed he'd evaded her question.

"Look, there's a patriotic program on this evening, fireworks and marching bands, you know, all the Fourth stuff. Wanna watch it?" He reached for her hand. "It's out of Washington. They usually put on a good show."

"Gosh, I'd forgotten about fireworks. What time?"

"Eight, I think. We'll check."

The stroll back to the cabin later that afternoon was like a nature study. Among the reeds at the lakeshore, they saw an oriole's nest, and a few feet beyond, a turtle cocked its head to gawk at them, then eased away. Goldenrods and daisies grew beside the trail.

"I think you'd make a good science teacher," Jeff said, seeming surprised at her knowledge of nature. "Ever considered it?"

"Science?" The research paper that Mr. Elgard assigned in high school came to mind. "Don't think so... well, might, who knows? I did study the horseshoe crab once."

Nestled together on the sofa that evening, they oohed and aahed at the fireworks with such color and splendor. "Have you ever seen so much color?" Persia commented as it ended. "Really cool. They outdid themselves this year."

"Quite pretty." He turned toward her with an amorous grin. "Right now I have my own fireworks in progress."

"Silly," she whispered and lifted her lips to his. "Me, too."

"Are you really gonna sleep upstairs? The bed's ready for you."

She looked at him strangely. "I thought that was the deal—that I'd take the upstairs bunk." She laughed.

"Deals are made to be broken, you know." He winked and pinched her arm playfully. Then kissed her again. "Please say you won't."

Without a word, she got up to slip upstairs to shower and change. By all means, she'd dab a touch of perfume on her wrists, too, and whatever happened, would happen, she told herself. Jeff was special. When might she ever have the chance to have a night alone with him again?

It was at least twenty minutes later that she hurried down the stairs, fresh and fragrant in red shorty pajamas. But where was Jeff? She tiptoed to the kitchen, then listened at the bathroom door… Surprised, she saw him in the bedroom sprawled, fully dressed, across the queen-sized bed—sound asleep! Without a word, she nestled down beside him, and totally comfortable, she let the night drift away.

CHAPTER 21

Finally, Louisville! The driver of the big rig turned right, and at Newburg Road Exit, Joe jumped out.

"Sure thank you," he yelled, his small frame feeling a jolt as he hit the pavement. Across the street, he hurried along Bishop Lane toward a Sonic sign. With little of the cash that Claudia had given him left, he ordered food and asked the man behind the counter how far it was to the racetrack, Churchill Downs.

"It's southwest of here. You'll need to go to 4th and Central. You can't miss it."

Joe took his order and stared at the man. "Could I walk? Is it far?"

"Might take a while. Yeah, you could."

Joe paid for the food—too burgers and fries—found a table away from the crowd, and proceeded to count his cash... twenty bucks! He'd eat and hitch a ride. The thought of the famous racetrack lured him like flies to molasses. At the corner of Central and Fourth, the drive let him out, took the six-dollar fare, and hurried away.

Joe, already awestruck, couldn't believe his eyes! The majestic grandstand, the track itself, and more flowers than he'd ever seen in one place was like a postcard setting. In front, he saw the main gate and, to his left, a row of what appeared to be stables or housing for horses… the backstretch or backside. The mere thought that one day he might actually get to race on that track made him glad all over! Everything about the place reflected racing, fun, and excitement, but where did he go to apply for work? A nearby shop caught his eye; he'd ask. An operation as large as Churchill Downs surely hired a lot of help, he told himself as he entered the shop, confident that employment awaited!

Inside, a man of medium build, ruddy skin, and balding leaned against the counter and held a paper. Behind the counter, a teenage girl glanced up when Joe entered, and the man with the paper quickly disappeared behind swinging doors. The room was quiet, almost deserted except for a lone man in the rear that sat as though waiting.

"Can I help you?" the young woman asked.

Joe stepped closer and said, "I hope to find work at the track. Can you tell me where I should go to apply? That's a mighty big place over there." He managed a grin and adjusted his shirt collar.

The young woman appeared surprised. "This is a vet's clinic. You need to—" She hesitated. "What kind of work? For the summer, you mean? You're out of school, I assume."

"Whatever I can find. I'm from California and I know a lot about horses. I thought I might find something, probably as a stable boy or groom. I can exercise… gallop horses, too. I even broke a mustang once…"

"Pardon me, but," she interrupted, "I can't tell you how they hire or who. I guess you'd need to go to the business office." She pointed to

143

the left. "Too bad you've come in mid-summer. Activity perks up in spring or fall."

"Do I go right or left?" Joe said, disappointed, and waited for directions!

The man at the back suddenly sprang forward and asked, "How old are you, son?"

"Fifteen, be sixteen next February."

"You need to go to the backside, the stables, and look, take my business card with you. It might help." The man handed him the card with the name *Hank Arnold, Trainer* on it.

"You're a trainer?" Joe could hardly believe it… what luck to meet a trainer so soon. Pure luck, he told himself.

"Retired, but yes, I know the ins and outs of that place. Show 'm this card and tell 'im I sent you. Try to find Rick Stubblefield. He's the one you need to see," the man added.

Joe's eyes widened. He could hardly believe it. "You know him?"

"Sure do. Great guy. He'll find something for you." The aging man seemed anxious for any recognition of his expertise.

"Thanks a lot. The backside, you say? I'm to go around thatta way?"

The man motioned as Joe stepped toward the door.

At the stables, Joe ambled along totally stunned at the facilities; all kinds of equipment and space for horses! The smell of hay, manure, and grooming supplies reminded him again of Whispering Trails— Claudia's place, and his friends in California. Roslynn, too, the way she giggled at stunts Rascal resorted to. Sure gave him a sense of home to go back to those memories. When would he ever move on to forget the happy days at Claudia's ranch?

"Rick Stubblefield?" the man at the gate asked when Joe showed him Hank Arnold's card. "Rick's in upper state New York. Took a colt up and won't return for a week."

"Not here, you say?"

"Sorry," the man said and walked away.

Joe's heart sank faster than a dead duck. All hopes of the connection faded, and with little or no cash in his pockets, he had no place to go... no money for food and no place to sleep!

At the intersection of 4th and Central, he passed a pedestrian. "Sir," he began. The man stopped. "Could you tell me how to get downtown?"

The man appeared startled. "The next street up is Third. It'll take you all the way downtown."

"Thanks," Joe muttered, devastated. One fact he'd learned of street life was that most homeless shelters were located in the downtown area of cities. Tired and disgruntled, he set out, wondering whether he'd made a mistake in coming to Louisville? Only time would tell. Another glance back at the track, and his doubts vanished. Louisville had horses—costly horses and trainers able to work with them, bring out the best in them. No, someway, somehow, he'd learn his way around; get to know the ropes of horseracing!

CHAPTER 22

LATER THAT DAY, JOE found the homeless shelter cleaner than most and comfortable; cots to sleep on and air conditioned, too! Fortunately, they served breakfast and it didn't take long for word to circulate that the parish house at the Cathedral of the Assumption gave out free lunches. With food taken care of, he spent much of the first day exploring Louisville—the riverfront, zoo, Old Louisville, and at Nelson Park he joined several loafers who, for one reason or another, had long aspired to race; would-be jocks, retired grooms, or trainers who either failed to get the chance or the horse that might carry them to fame. Certainly, with dreams unfulfilled, their lives now turned to spinning the best possible yarns that sometimes stretched beyond reason. Their stories, interesting and colorful, did make for good listening! Joe made it a point to join them in the hope that some part of it might rub off on him!

The week passed, and Rick Stubblefield, a tall, lean man of fifty, graying at the temples and weathered, returned but offered little in the way of encouragement. He spoke bluntly and to the point. When Joe handed him the business card, he noticed Rick had a twitch at the corner of his left eye. "This man thought you might have a job that I could do," Joe said. Intimidated already by Rick's demeanor, Joe glanced away so as not to make eye contact.

"Hank Arnold? Where'd you meet this guy?" Rick mumbled from the side of his mouth.

"Said he was a retired trainer. I met 'im over at the clinic across the street."

"Don't have no idea who he is, but look, I do need a stable boy," he finally said. "For the summer, I assume. How old are you?"

"Fifteen."

"Go to school, I guess."

"Yeah. It's out for the summer, though." Joe realized he'd conveniently lied again.

"You've mucked stables before?"

"Yes, sir. I lived on a ranch out in California. Rode daily, even broke a wild mustang or two."

"So what brings you to Louisville?"

"Like horses—like 'em a lot. Like to ride, exercise, well, anything really. I'd like to become a jockey, but you know how that goes."

Rick Stubblefield appeared to listen, occasionally nodded or grimaced, and soon asked Joe to follow him for a look at the stables.

From that time on, the two of them spoke little. Rick spent much of the time with a thoroughbred named *Gravi Train*, and Joe, though bored with his menial task of mucking and such, told himself that some work was better than none. In a mere few days he'd be able to find a place to live and shop for new clothes. If his work pleased Rick, he might allow him to breeze the thoroughbred or become his official exercise rider, and each day as he walked the distance from the track north on Third Street to the downtown shelter, he dreamed of better times to come.

* * *   * * *   * * *

Three weeks passed during which Joe and Rick seldom interacted. At times, Joe wondered whether his work was satisfactory or if Rick as much as liked having him around. He tried not to think about it or about Whispering Trails in California but went about his menial tasks, careful always to pitch dry straw into each stable as Chub at Claudia's had instructed.

"Joe." It was Rick one morning in late May.

Joe stopped his work and faced his boss. "Yes, sir," he muttered as he threw down an extra handful of straw. Had he done something wrong?

"I'm in a squeeze." Rick's twitch was more pronounced as he grimaced. "My exercise rider is leaving for Dallas. He has accepted a new job out there."

"Yes, sir."

"And the owner of *Gravi Train* is flying in tomorrow."

"From Dallas?"

"No, Bristow, Oklahoma. He wants me to enter Gravi in the Kennicott Classic at Farmington in six weeks. It's the last race of the spring meet... early July."

"Oklahoma?" Joe cocked his head to the side.

"But I'm not sure the colt's ready. Trouble is Ed Blasingame won't take *no* for an answer. He's puttin' plenty of pressure on me."

"But you're the trainer. You oughta know what the horse can do."

"But these owners want action. Fast action. Did you tell me that you'd worked with horses in California? Breezed and exercised 'em at some ranch out there?"

"Sure did. Yeah, I've worked with thoroughbreds, too... with a trainer on the premises." Joe squared his shoulders proudly.

Rick stared into Joe's boyish face. "Wanna try your hand with Gravi? See what he'll do for you? The colt needs exercise."

"When's the owner to come?"

"Tomorrow from Oklahoma."

"I lived in Oklahoma for a while—Duncan."

"Yeah, Blasingame owns an oil company out there. The rich kind," Rick said and ran his hand through his thinning hair.

Joe felt like shouting! Finally a chance to ride! "I'm not sure where Bristow is."

"Just west of Tulsa. I grew up at Claremore myself."

"You did? Small world," Joe said, not ready for Rick's life story. His heart was on Gravi!

The bay colt was pretty; good form, sleek, and shiny coat, and long legs. Joe placed his foot in the iron to pull himself into the saddle, happier than a bride at the altar!

Rick watched as Joe's small legs fit close to the mount's shoulders, his head high and hands gripping the reins to quickly whiz off down the famous track on Gravi Train, the thoroughbred with an Oklahoma connection!

For Joe, it was pure exhilaration as he felt the colt's strong movement beneath him and the wind in his face. At the onset, he whacked the colt on the rump and felt him plunge forward, then even out into his own pace. What a way to make the day!

At the first turn of the mile-long oval, he urged Gravi on—and bent low to whisper, "Go home for me, boy. Let's go." He felt the colt's strong muscles contract, then push forward to finish at 1.12, not record-breaking time, but good practice... mighty good practice, Joe told himself.

At the gate, Rick met him with a wide grin. "Good going... you got him to go. I think the colt likes you."

"He's got speed. You've got yourself a winner," Joe commented.

"But racing 'im in six weeks?"

"Sure won't hurt to try... with plenty of good workouts between now and then."

* * * * * * * * *

A week later when Joe received his first paycheck, he confronted Rick regarding a place to live. "If I'm to work the horse each morning," he began, "I need to live closer in. Know of a good apartment around here?"

"Come with me," Rick said and led Joe through several hallways to a small area near the tack shop. "I slept here myself for a few nights. Can't beat it for convenience."

Joe glanced around the space not much larger than a modern bathroom, already furnished with a twin-sized bed, small, table-model TV, microwave oven next to an inset bath. He immediately thought of his place at Claudia's, but didn't comment.

"Big enough?" Rick asked.

"How much?"

"Free of charge. You're aware that the venders at the grandstand sell all kinds of food."

"I know. Seen it already, but also found the stairs to the jockey's room."

"Sounds like you've looked into this place," Rick said and smiled.

"On the first day," Joe said with a chuckle. "Say, how old do you have to be to become a jockey?"

"Sixteen, I guess. You might ask around," Rick mumbled before he walked away.

Joe, totally beside himself, had his own thoughts. Louisville had come through for him, but somehow he wondered if it'd last. Fate had served him some pretty hard blows already. Would it prove different this time?

CHAPTER 23

SEPTEMBER BROUGHT COOLER DAYS to Pittsburgh. Compared to Oklahoma, fall weather came earlier. Persia noticed some early tinges of color in the gardens, too; trees showed red and yellow, occasional blades of grass appeared drier, and most of the summer annuals had quit blooming.

Jeff even noticed the difference. "You must feel like a kid out of a book who skips through a wonderland of color," he'd commented with a chuckle. Actually, she'd seen little of him of late. "Down right disgusting," she mumbled at times when he failed to call. With his work at Wesco and the law classes, he had no spare time, or so he'd said. He *had* made it down often throughout the summer—had attended her fall sorority dance, too, when they'd danced the night away dressed in formal attire. Oh, he looked handsome! All the girls ooh and aahed over him—his good looks! Of all their dates, that occasion topped the list. And, of course, there was the weekend at his parents' cabin. To think of it still made her giggle.

At times, she wondered if she didn't feel too deeply for him, too serious; something about him gave her anxiety. But her schoolwork helped… kept her busy. Usually, her morning classes at the university ended by 1:00, but other assignments such as library and reading, took additional time, sometimes as much as five or six hours. The solitude was always calming; time to think. It wasn't unusual for her, while seated in a far-corner cubicle, to escape to her own thoughts—thoughts of Joe Dee and her biological mother, days at the old trailer court in Oklahoma. Sometimes, amid all the glamour of Clairmont, she pondered her present life and how it had changed. What she wouldn't give to see them again, especially Joe Dee. It wasn't that she didn't love Mama, just couldn't understand her willingness to sign away her children. Persia got up from the chair and stepped to the window. "Guess I shouldn't judge Mama. Guess she thought it was her best option at the time. Adults do strange things at times. Just like Bebe—already involved with another woman! I could work him over with words, but what good would it do? She raked her hand across her brow, disgusted. Do no good at all! She picked up a book and began to read again.

* * * *   * * * *   * * * *

Two weeks passed, two busy weeks! At times, she felt as though September was a dream; football season social life at school, and work! Certainly, a whirlwind of dances, parties, and games; too much to have time to worry when Jeff failed to call. And with her sorority's fundraiser, a carwash for abused children, only two weeks away she felt a new sense of purpose, even giddy. Placards, ads, and radio announcements to do, not to mention an essay in English comp class! "Good gosh, Jill," she complained to her friend. "I'm spread thinner than goat's pee." The two had become friends as sorority sisters.

"But we have to hang in there. We have to put this project over. Our sorority came in second last year," Jill Douglas responded with a frown. "We want to win this time."

"Don't worry, I'll make—wouldn't miss it, even if that essay is late."

* * * *   * * * *   * * * *

As planned, two weeks later the girls, clad in jeans and tees, assembled for the big event! Persia, with her hair pulled back in a ponytail, dabbed scads of sunscreen on and left the house in a whiz.

Already, a string of vehicles circled the huge parking lot ready for a wash. With all the giggling, squeals, and loud talk, the girls worked feverishly to lure motorists in for "a fabulous carwash for a mere five bucks." Often in the process, they accidentally sprayed one another instead of an oncoming car, producing more giggles, shouts, and laughter until the entire area teemed with fun and boisterous activity.

"Hi," a young customer greeted as he approached for a wash. "Ya'll do a good job, now," he teased, his blond hair wind-blown and dangling on his brow.

Persia took the hose and hurried to spray and scrub the dust from his car, the sides first, then the rear, when she noticed his license plate. "You from Texas?" she yelled and stepped toward the passenger's side for his reply.

"Nope, just moved here. Haven't had time to change my tag."

"Oh." She continued to wipe the doors of the vehicle.

"Why do you ask?"

"I lived in Oklahoma once—years ago. Just wondered."

"Where in Oklahoma?" His amber eyes lit up with a boyish grin. He appeared to be no more than fifteen or sixteen.

"I think near Lawton. Know where that is?"

"Heard of it." He appeared surprised.

She studied his features. "What's your name?"

"Butch Tanner."

"B—Butch Tanner? Have you always gone by that name?"

He appeared puzzled. "Reckon so. Nobody ever told me different." He chuckled. "Look, gotta go if you're finished."

"Hurry, Persia," one girl yelled. "You're holding up traffic."

"Okay." She watched the young kid with the Texas plates drive away. "Guess he thought I was nuts," she mumbled to her friend just as someone rushed up and gave her a sudden shower with the hose. "You need coolin' off."

"Just you wait. Your time's coming," she yelled with a shout of laughter. "Stop it."

And who appeared next? Jeff. She eagerly rushed to greet him, surprised. "How'd you find me?"

"Your housekeeper told me." He grinned flirtatiously. "Go to work, gal, and do a bang-up job. You hear?"

"Ah, hush. Where've you been so long?" She didn't wait for an answer. "Want your car washed?"

"Yes, and more."

"Like what, may I ask?"

"Why don't we have dinner this evening?" Their eyes met in a romantic connection.

Her heart pounded. "Look at me. Do I look like dinner? Why didn't you call earlier? I'm a wreck and I won't get home until late this afternoon."

"Just whizzed into town and thought we might get together." He glanced away.

"I can't, Jeff. We're busy here, but look, roll up your window and I'll give you a splash, give you an A+ car wash." She managed to laugh. Should she have accepted?

She watched his expression turn somber, even glum, and soon the car was as shiny as new. He rolled down the window slightly and handed her a five-dollar bill. Before she could say more, he whizzed away.

"Wasn't that Jeff Lorton?" Jill Douglas said later.

"Yeah, guess I gave him the cold shoulder. I'm mad at myself, too."

"Why? You like 'im, don't you?"

"That's the problem. I think he's taking me for granted. Why couldn't he have called ahead? That'll teach 'im."

"Oh," Jill grunted as another car drove up. "That'll teach 'im," Jill repeated.

The project proceeded and Persia worried. She would probably never see Jeff again.

In all, the carwash netted $4,000—more than any campus drive in history, but when the day ended, Persia went home exhausted both physically and mentally... even depressed. Jeff's appearance spoiled her day. Why did he come? And the young man with the Texas license plate—the kid with blond hair and amber eyes. "Might Joe Dee look something like that boy now?" Was it possible that her brother had been adopted earlier and had his name changed? Sometimes adoptees do, such as herself for an example. "I'm fantasizing again," she told herself just as the phone rang.

"Sweetie?" It was Bebe calling. "I'm coming home Monday."

"Alone?"

"I have a doctor's appointment on Tuesday. I've experienced some gastric problems lately—can't keep my food down. Thought I'd better have Dr. Levy check me over."

Persia felt her own stomach knot. "You're sick, Bebe?"

"Could be a virus. He'll get to the bottom of it."

"A virus?" she managed to ask.

"Let's hope that's all it is."

"I'm worried, Bebe," she whispered into the phone. "Are you sure you're gonna be okay?"

"I'm sure, honey. Now don't worry," he assured her as they ended the call.

CHAPTER 24

J OE HARTSONG LOVED LOUISVILLE—THE best place on earth, he told himself almost daily! Even better than Claudia's ranch, Whispering Trails, out in California. Well, except Rick Stubblefield, his boss, didn't possess Claudia's sweet, friendly disposition. He could be as cantankerous as a mule when things didn't go to suit 'im. Probably just have to take 'im as he is, Joe decided, determined not to let him discourage him too much. Kentucky was horse country; it'd be totally foolish to leave. Besides, Gravi Train, the oil man's three-year-old colt, showed promise. Something good was bound to come of that horse, just bound to, Joe told himself as he got out of bed ready to hit the track for the morning exercise ritual.

"Wait, Joe. Got a minute?" Rick yelled when he saw Joe outside Gravi's stable.

"Sure, what's up?"

"I'm making you foreman," Rick said as he stepped toward Joe with his head bowed as if in deep thought.

Joe's pulse raced, his muscles tightened. "M—me?" he stammered, totally shocked. Finally Rick showed some confidence in him. What had come over him? He seemed so sullen at times.

"Ben's headin' out tomorrow. Goin' to California. Some trainer out there offered 'im a good deal."

"Where in California?"

"Not sure. Some ranch outside L.A. is all he told me, and I didn't ask." Rick Stubblefield knew horses, and he knew racetracks all over, too. "Guess it's somewhere near Santa Anita would be my guess."

"Bet so," Joe answered and raked his tawny hair to the side. "Tell ya one thing. Gravi's sure picked up speed lately. That colt can run when you know how to get it out of 'im." Joe grinned proudly, aware that he was the colt's only exercise rider. He must've done something right.

"Guess our Bristow friend'll be mighty pleased to hear that," Rick muttered with his usual guttural chuckle.

"Yep, I think Gravi knows me, too. Responds well. I'm proud of 'im."

Rick flashed another grin and turned to go. "Keep up the good work, and by the way, I'm raising your pay. How does a hundred more per week sound?" He winked. "Think you can use it?"

"You bet, and thanks." Joe felt his face flush with glee. "Thanks a lot." He watched as Rick disappeared around the corner.

The next morning, Joe was up early, eager to breeze Gravi around the track with the first orange glow of sunrise. The pay raise gave him an eagerness to please Rick even more, and for the coming weeks, he'd make sure the colt got plenty of workouts, each time pushing Gravi just a little harder—raising expectations. With the warm southern temperatures that sometimes reminded him of California and the strong rhythmic movements of Gravi under him, he felt a certain exhilaration that for months had escaped him. Even fond memories of Claudia and Roslynn in California faded somewhat as runs with Gravi increased. Life moves on, he told himself, and as far as he was concerned, he'd moved his tack (as the big boys called it) to Louisville, and that's where he'd stay. Next May, he'd be right there, too, for the Derby, and he couldn't wait! Nothing on this side of the moon would prevent it. In fact, the mere thought of it thrilled him tremendously. Yep, Kentucky was horse country!

As the hot of summer gradually passed and the stronger gust of autumn blew in, Joe felt a new sense of self... freedom with money to spend. Better food from local cafés, too, and an occasional movie when time permitted. By late September, Churchill Downs held no mysteries; he knew the place from one side to the other. He'd explored every inch, the stables, the grandstand, had even peered into the windows of the jockeys' room. One day when his courage surged, he'd go up, tap on the door, and ask some questions—how does a fella break into racing? How did one get his name before the public, or out to the owners? But with no formal experience, well, other than amateur riding, he feared the well-established jocks might ignore him, especially with so many grooms, trainers, and exercise riders far more expert than he available at any given time.

Still, with the fall meet some over a month away, why not ask to ride as a jockey in some of the daily races? With his experience at Claudia's, he surely possessed the knowledge for that. "If I can only play my cards right with Rick," he mumbled, dashing out of his sleeping quarters, "he might help me arrange it. Everybody here knows Rick. He might just make a few connections for me." With the idea in mind, his spirits soared with a new determination not to give up.

* * * *　* * * *　* * * *

Two weeks passed, and the fall racing meet was even closer when Joe mustered the courage. Yep, he'd visit the jockeys' room! Nervously, he climbed the stairs, anxious to knock. At the top of the stairs, he stood for a moment hoping to calm down. Should he or shouldn't he? Rumor had it that few visitors frequented this place—some of the jockeys might be undressed, just out of the shower, or engrossed in a card game, all of which sounded fun, but how did a fella get accepted? It was worth a try. He tapped on the door and anxiously waited.

"Can I help you?" a man of hardly five feet tall and a hundred pounds asked when he opened the door.

"I'm looking for Le Carlo Montez," Joe nervously uttered in the hope that the fake name sounded authentic; it was the first name that came to mind.

"Here? He's supposed to be here?" the jockey asked. "I don't know anyone by that name. I'm Gil Richards. Are you sure he comes here?"

"I thought so. My name's Joe Hartsong. I'm Rick Stubblefield's foreman over at the backside… the stables. My dream is to become a jockey, and Montez said he'd talk with me about it, give me some advice."

"What was it you wanted to know? Maybe I can help."

"Just general information, really, such as how old I'd need to be to race and how to break in."

"Sixteen, at least, and just find somebody, some owner who'll let you ride. It's as simple as that. There's a maiden race for every jockey and a maiden race for every horse." He grinned. "It's a hard road, my friend. Get ready for a lot of disappointments. Some refer to us jockeys as dream chasers, but I guess you could say that about anything worth doing." Gil Richard's face brightened so that lines showed at the corners of his eyes. He must have been forty years of age. "Try racing in some midling races, minors, before tackling the big ones. You'll improve your résumé that way," Gil continued.

Joe thanked him and descended the stairs more determined than ever. His dream of becoming a jockey was definitely fixed, and with such good advice, he realized he needed to spend more time in the jockeys' room. With his experience with Gravi Train and the fact that Rick had entrusted him as foreman, he wasn't a complete novice. He needed to pal around with those boys, the jockeys, as much as possible, he decided as another idea hit.

Rick had recently certified Gravi for the New Mexico Winter Classic for February. Again, if he played his cards right, Rick might just ask him to ride Gravi for the race. After all, he breezed and galloped the colt more than anyone else. And with the fall meet ahead, why not ask him to enter the colt on the daily program for some races there at the track. Of course, Rick, as trainer, would make the decision. It surely wouldn't hurt to ask, Joe told himself, eager to make a name for himself. If he and Gravi made a good team, Rick might be more apt to consider him good enough for New Mexico.

At the backside later, he leaned against the fence, captivated by the idea. Sixteen? No problem. He'd have his sixteenth birthday in two months, plenty of time for the big race. He picked up a pebble, then tossed it down, sure his plan could work. But Rick might just shrug it off as fantasy... he was under great pressure from the oil tycoon in Oklahoma, no doubt about it. Still, he might just see it his way; Rick could be softhearted at times. Joe picked up another stone and tossed it. For now, he'd take Gil Richards advice and try for midling races on weekends. It wouldn't hurt and certainly would improve his racing experience!

CHAPTER 25

NOVEMBER CAME AND JOE still hadn't confronted Rick regarding Gravi's maiden race… the New Mexico Classic. It was a major race and Rick was under pressure from the Oklahoma oil man to show the colt off; make a name for himself and the horse. Rick realized, too, that Joe was a rookie at racing, though he'd been chosen to participate in two daily races at the track. Someone noticed his success with Gravi and passed the word that he, more than anyone else, could get the best from the colt. Though neither race won, the mere notice of his name on the program sent his ego soaring! Grooms and exercise riders spoke more frequently, sought his advice, and even trips to the jockeys' room became more frequent.

"You'll need an agent," one jockey advised one day as he dealt a new hand at cards. "An agent negotiates for you. He'll get your name out before the public, especially to owners. They're the main cog in the wheel—they purchase the horses." He chuckled. "With big bucks."

It all sounded like Greek to him, but Joe realized the jock knew the business. "I wouldn't know where to start," he mumbled as he tried to absorb every detail. "Wouldn't know where to find an agent." Sometimes he felt like a goose in a henhouse. The other jockeys got big offers to ride for big stakes while he sat on the sidelines like a schoolboy at a ballgame. But as Chub, his former boss at Claudia's, had said, "Anything worthwhile comes high; nothing worthwhile comes without effort." An image of Chub flashed before him, stout, muscular, and plenty strict. Just like Mr. Murphy down in Duncan had been. A good man, Mr. Murphy was, well, except when he up and sold my horse, Joe remembered. Never been able to understand why he did it, even if my grades did drop. A knock on the tack shop door interrupted his reminiscence.

It was Rick in tee-shirt and jeans. "Mr. Murdock's coming to check on his colt," Rick said with a furrowed brow. "How's the colt doing?"

"I'd say better than usual—up to doing the oval in 1:25, which is pretty darn good if you ask me."

"Murdock's to get here by 8:30 tomorrow morning. He's flying in from Tulsa. Let's forego the exercise session for tomorrow and run the colt after he arrives." His voice almost cracked. "Don't wanna tire the colt beforehand... and do have 'im groomed, coat glossy. Curry 'im good and untangle the points. Show 'im up good." Rick pursed his lips for emphasis.

"Yes, sir... uh, Rick, I was wondering at the possibility of me ridin' Gravi in New Mexico. Reckon Mr. Murdock might allow it? I know his colt better'n... well, I know 'im well. Could you suggest it to 'im while he's here?"

Rick didn't answer, except with a mumbled, "A lot's at stake here," and he turned to go.

Joe jerked on his shoes to go to the stable. Mr. Murdock, the rich man from Oklahoma, was flying in, and according to Rick, had already certified Gravi for the upcoming New Mexico Classic. If the colt performed to his satisfaction, he just might ask him to be in the irons for the race. Logically, he was the most qualified rider, by far. He'd spent more time with the colt than anyone. Whether Mr. Murdock was aware of that fact was anybody's guess. A good performance might do the trick. The prospect totally blew him away! A real career as a jockey might be rising on the horizon! Joe took a deep breath and headed toward Gravi's stable, ready to work magic on the colt… clean 'im up fancy.

By the time the morning passed, Gravi was all curried and clean. His coat shone like satin and his full, flowing tail and mane were free of tangles. Joe stood back to admire his job; he'd never seen the colt look better!

* * * * * * * * *

Mr. Murdock arrived as scheduled the next morning, obviously proud of his horse. A short, stubby man, his friendly yet businesslike manner made it easy to converse.

"Glad to meecha, sir," Joe said when Rick introduced them. "Got a mighty fine colt here. I'm his exercise rider."

Murdock's keen eyes got a glint; his heavy jowls waddled when he chuckled. "How's he doing? Can he run?"

"Good. Plenty of speed." Joe noticed the man's shiny brown boots under his trouser legs and a tweed sports jacket that must have cost plenty, not to mention a fine Stetson on his head.

"Wanna see 'im run?" Joe said as he fastened the girth about Gravi and set his foot in the iron to pull himself up. With a tug on the reins and a slight push against the flanks, they were off. Gravi lunged to Joe's delight and sped off as fast as a bullet! With his boots close to the colt's shoulders, Joe concentrated on the track ahead. "Come on, boy," he coaxed as he leaned low toward the colt's ear. "Let's show the man what we can do. Do me proud, Gravi. Come on, boy, let's go," he coaxed, and was off around the track.

Whether Gravi misunderstood Joe's request or just wasn't in the mood, after several seconds, the colt slowed... slowed more, balked and refused to go! Finally, Joe managed to make the track at 1:44, which fell well below expectations. Devastated, his spirits fell as well! A knot rose in his throat; he wanted to vomit, jump off the colt and hide. What on earth came over Gravi? What was his problem? Leading the horse back to the stable with his head down, Joe realized that any hope that he might ride the colt in New Mexico vanished. Rick and Mr. Murdock stood with their heads together, obviously disappointed.

"What happened?" Rick snapped as he stepped toward Joe, his brow furrowed and his face flushed.

"The colt, sir, for once refused to run... couldn't get a darn thing outta 'im. Kept balking on me," Joe mumbled, embarrassed. "I've never seen 'im do so bad."

"How long you been ridin', boy?" the owner snapped, obviously devastated.

"Long time, sir. Gravi can do a hundred times better'n this. Sorry to disappoint ya."

Rick interrupted. "Joe's done a lot better with your colt, sir. Sorry he didn't demonstrate the horse's progress this time. I assure you Gravi is improving. One day he'll be a good racehorse."

With Gravi back in the stable, Rick and his visitor soon disappeared into Rick's office. Joe imagined they were both furious. He wanted to sneak away to his small quarters in the tack shop and sulk. Not since his childhood had he felt so alone—like he could cry. "Failure again," he mumbled, embarrassed, "and to think, I'll have to face the jockeys at another card game."

CHAPTER 26

THEIR PATHS SELDOM CROSSED during the next two weeks; Joe continued his work with the colt and Rick had little to say. More than once Joe thought of leaving—to where he had no idea. Louisville seemed like home. He loved the atmosphere. And even if his acquaintances seldom came around anymore, he somehow held on to the dream of becoming a jockey. If he couldn't make it in Louisville, where? Visitors came from all over to see the famous racetrack where top-pedigreed thoroughbreds were often boarded for months under the supervision of some of the best trainers in the business. Yet, Joe with all his tenacity and willingness to learn realized he'd failed. He was getting nowhere, which often threw him into bouts of despair and anguish.

His relationship with Gravi suffered, too. Not that he blamed the colt for the poor performance before the Bristow oilman, but subconsciously it was difficult to put the same confidence in the colt that disappointed him so terribly at the very time when he needed to make a good impression. He and Gravi had been a team for months, and each time the colt had responded beautifully… just hard to understand, Joe mused, as he tried desperately to put it behind him.

* * * *   * * * *   * * * *

It was mid-November when he dressed one morning and left his room in the tack shop to go about his daily routine when Rick and a stranger, a man of small stature and graying at the temples, spoke when he passed them. Joe breezed by not intending to stop.

"Joe, this is Toby Ingles, who will ride Gravi Train in the February Classic in New Mexico. Do you have any suggestions for 'im regarding the colt?"

So Rick had already found a jockey for the race, Joe mulled. Didn't even so much as ask my opinion. He managed to grin at the stranger and extended his hand. "Nice to meecha. Nothing here, except you'll have a mighty fine horse to ride," Joe mumbled, not too happy.

"Joe's done most of the work with Gravi—under my supervision, of course. He's had good results, too," Rick said with a cheerful grin.

"Well, except when his owner showed up," Joe said, managing to chuckle. "Never did understand why the colt let me down the way he did—balked on me, totally balked, and he'd never done it before." Joe shook his head and noticed Rick grimaced.

Whatever Toby Ingles thought he kept to himself except to say, "He probably took a stubborn streak." They laughed.

"He'll do fine for you, and I wish you well," Joe added, about to go.

"Don't bother to work 'im out this morning," Rick said to Joe. "Toby might want to do it himself, get familiar with 'im."

Joe agreed and turned to go and leave the two men to their business. What was he to say? Rick knew he wanted to ride Gravi in the February race, but didn't so much as discuss the options. "Darn." Joe bit his lip to keep from blurting something obnoxious. Again, he thought of leaving Louisville, just downright leaving Rick where he'd found him. But what would that prove? He wondered whether he'd ever be able to trust Rick again. Certainly, for the past few weeks their relationship had gone downhill. Sadly, Joe returned to his room and kicked off his boots. A flip of the radio knob brought loud music, some rock band out of Chicago. The entire day loomed ahead with nothing on hand. Why not go downtown to Nelson Park and hang out a while, meet with friends?

Suddenly, he heard a tap on the door. Had someone knocked? Rick, probably, with more questions for that blasted jockey. I'm going to tell Rick he can go where it don't snow," Joe fussed. "Of all the favors he could've given me—the chance to ride Gravi in the New Mexico Classic—he ups and gets somebody else. Sure was a letdown, too. He ambled to the door and opened it.

Surprisingly, Wendi Wohl stood before him and held an envelope. "Someone sent this letter over here," she began. "It has your name on it." Wendi came to the backside on Tuesdays and Thursdays to exercise a bay colt named "First Waltz."

"A letter… for me? Who, for gosh sakes?"

"Yeah, has *Joe Hartsong* on it. It's from California."

"California? Can't be." He tore the envelope open as Wendi turned to go. "Thanks," he yelled and began to examine the contents. "Whispering Trails" was printed on the stationery. Claudia McClish, no doubt, but why? What did she have to say after so long a time?

"High Pockets hasn't lived up to my expectations," she wrote. "The colt is three now and has won only three races—local races at

171

that. When I read your name in a bio of Rick Stubblefield in a racing magazine recently, I knew I had to contact you."

Joe frowned. "Contact me?" he muttered, confused. "Why?"

"I remembered that you had a way with my colt, got more out of him that anyone, and may I offer my sincere apology for dismissing you, Joe. I was in a frenzy, a state of anxiety regarding Roslynn, my godchild. She is well and doing fine. My question to you is this. If I can get High Pockets certified for the Derby next May and send him on to Louisville in the near future, will you work with him in the hope that the colt might at least show in the race? I have spent millions on the horse and would like to have some recompense for money spent. By the way, Roslynn sends her good wishes."

Joe reread the letter. Of all the surprises that might have come his way, this topped them all. Claudia, of all people, had located him, apologized, and to top it all had asked him to see that her prized thoroughbred was prepared to run in the Derby in some over six months. Tall order, he told himself. If the horse had won only two local races, how could she expect him to qualify for such a famous race? Should he refuse? He'd have to think through this. He stuck the letter in his pocket and left.

At 1:00, racing began at the track and a crowd assembled. It was always fun to see the rush to the rail as the ponies came around toward the finish line. No thrill like it, Joe thought, especially when I'm in the irons! The thought that one day he might don the bright-colored silks and riding boots buoyed his spirits… Claudia, of all people, has faith in me. The idea hit him like a tonic! My dear friend Claudia—nobody like her!

That evening, he re-opened Claudia's letter and read it. In his mind, he saw her clear blue yes, gorgeous premature silvery hair—Claudia was in her early forties and didn't look a day over thirty. She'd been good to him, gave him a home when he was down on his luck. No, he couldn't refuse her request. Whatever might happen regarding her horse, well, he'd make no promises. Both he and High Pockets seemed on equal par… failures! One more couldn't put either any lower. He got up, stepped to a nearby phone, and placed a call to the enclosed number!

"Claudia, Joe. Gotcha letter. How's everybody doing?"

"Great, Joe. So glad you called. We miss you."

"You say you're thinking of sending High Pockets to Louisville?"

"It's an idea. What do you think?" She hesitated. "That colt has been nothing but disappointment. I had great plans for him. After the costs he's been, I have nothing to praise him for. He has won a few minor races, but that's all."

"Chub still with you? What does he think?"

"No, I think he gave up and moved on to Montana." She laughed. "Think there's any hope?"

"Guess it won't hurt to try. You realize I'm no trainer."

"But you have worked with High Pockets—know his weaknesses and strengths, if he has any." She laughed again. "Besides, I think you might have a special interest in the colt; we were all like family once."

"Yeah, I hated to leave, Claudia. I might add, though, that since that time I've moved here and have never enjoyed a place more… decided to become a jockey, Claudia. How does that sound?" he laughed. "But I've had my own failures, disappointments. Yeah, plenty of 'em."

"Jockey, you say?"

"Yep, my heart's set on it. They tell me it's a struggle, though."

"How exciting. Listen, kid. You get my colt in shape and you'll have plenty of offers for the irons." She laughed. "I mean it. We'll work together on this." She'd never sounded more upbeat.

Joe didn't put much faith in her statement; Claudia was interested in her horse, it was obvious. And like others who'd promised to help, she could let him down, too. Yet, Claudia did have a good heart. To do her a favor wouldn't hurt. Yeah, he'd work with her horse and consider it his good deed for the year. He smiled and asked her to send the horse on.

High Pockets arrived a week later with instructions that trainer Dan Wakenmeyer was to be in charge. The three-year-old had matured over the past months; stronger, longer legs, good stance, and the glossiest coat ever. Joe rubbed his hand across the colt's shoulder and spoke his name. High Pockets responded with a movement of the upper lip. Joe remembered from Rusty, his Oklahoma horse, that it was a signal of acknowledgement. "Good boy," Joe whispered, thrilled to see the colt again. "We'll show some folks what we can do," he added before joining Dan for coffee. The reconnection with Claudia McClish felt good. He'd do what he could; he felt like he owed it to her for giving him a home and employment when he had no place to go. The least he could do was to repay a good friend.

CHAPTER 27

NOVEMBER CAME COLD AND troubling at Clairmont. Uncertainly ran rampant. B. W.'s doctor's appointment in late September resulted in a diagnosis of colon cancer. He'd undergone surgery three days earlier. Nine inches of his colon were removed. Persia missed three days of classes to sit by his side at the hospital, often holding his hand or wiping his brow. The thought of losing another parent, especially Bebe, upset her terribly. He was her rock, her security, and since Mumsy died—even with disagreements regarding Sherri Tahlwald—it was Bebe who she knew held the reins to her future. Without him, what?

Something about the astute businessman never gave up. When his discharge from the hospital came, B. W. calmly relocated to the library at Clairmont and went about work as usual. "I'm fine, sweetie. Go about your own schedule," he'd say. "Patsy will see to my needs." Patsy was the private nurse hired to attend to his convalescence.

"But, Bebe, are you sure you're okay? Does anything hurt?" Persia probed. She knew Bebe, knew how he sometimes hid reality. Even his medical team had failed to disclose the extent of the cancer. Had it spread, metastasized? More than once since his surgery, she'd cried herself to sleep. Needless to say, fall was anything but pleasant. Even her grades at school dropped from A's to B's, and her relationship with Jeff showed signs of cooling. With Thanksgiving only three weeks away, any chance of seeing him any time soon seemed bleak. Sadly enough, she might say the same regarding Bebe. Once he was well, he'd fly right back to Palm Beach—he'd say to transact business, but if she were guessing, it would be to see Sherri. Oh, she'd like to give that woman a piece of her mind… tell her to go on about her life and leave Bebe alone! She wouldn't, though. What if Bebe got sick again… really sick, or died? She'd never forgive herself. No, she'd leave well enough alone.

Upstairs in her room, she stepped to the window. Outside, strong fall gusts sent leaves dancing down like tiny spaceships hovering over landing sites. It seemed ages since her last connection with Molly, who was in school at Northwestern. Surely, she'd come home for the holidays. And Jeff? Three weeks had passed without a word. What excuse might he resurrect next time? Or would he even bother to call at all? Wish Bebe would feel better soon, she mumbled as the telephone rang.

"Hello," she answered, hoping to hear Jeff's voice.

"Persia?" It was he, of all people.

Shocked, she wondered how to respond after so long. "Hi, Jeff," she finally said. "Whatcha doin'?"

"What do you have planned for Friday evening? Remember, you told me to call in advance?" He chuckled. "I'm following orders."

"Yep, sure did," she replied flippantly, determined not to show disappointment that he hadn't called sooner.

"I'm to be in Pittsburgh this weekend and thought we could touch base. It has been a while."

Oh, gosh, what was she to say? "Uh, Friday evening, you say?"

"Can you make it?" His voice sounded pleasant and friendly. "Have you recovered from the carwash?"

"That was weeks ago. I'm fine. Finally got some rest." She hesitated. "What time Friday evening... for dinner, you mean?"

"Yes. Is seven okay?"

"Sounds good," she said as calmly as she could muster. Of course, she wanted to see Jeff. She'd missed him terribly. Her heart raced happily. "Thanks, Jeff. Thanks for calling," she said as she said goodbye.

"Needless to say, I like this place," Jeff said at the Reflections Friday evening as they entered the restaurant. "I like the atmosphere here."

"Me, too... the aura," Persia responded as they took seats near a window. "Food's good, too. I'm hungry." She flashed a big smile and flipped her hair flirtatiously.

From across the table, she studied his face—the expressive eyes, nice lips that parted sensually into a warm thoughtful smile, and his thick flaxen hair always perfectly coiffed... that's Jeff, she thought. What woman wouldn't fall for him? If only she knew what went on in that head of his. Did he have romantic interests elsewhere? Was he really as busy as he pretended?

"How's your dad?" he asked after they ordered.

"Back at work, I suppose. He left yesterday for Florida. Haven't heard from him since. I guess everything's fine."

"Did he tell you that I dropped in to see him when he had his surgery?"

"No, where was I?"

"At school, I suppose. We visited mainly about business. He seemed in good spirits."

"I think my dad has a one-track mind most of the time." She laughed. "I hope he didn't talk your socks off."

The conversation ran from school, her classes at the university, to his work and law classes. A few times during the meal, he reflected on his own family and how he missed his mom, especially with the holidays ahead, at which time Persia mentioned Mumsy and special times with her, also.

"Wanna drive down by the river?" he asked as they walked to the car later. A few flakes of snow balleted before them like tiny ballerinas in fancy tutus.

"Are you sure we won't freeze?" Persia asked, taking his arm.

"My car is equipped with a heater," he quipped facetiously. "Ever hear of an arm-strong heater? Got one of those, too." He hugged her and winked.

"My, aren't you witty tonight?"

He started the car as the snow fell thicker. "This may serve as a sleigh ride except we don't have a horse," he whispered. "Come closer. Sit by me. Keep me warm." He took her arm and pulled her over.

"Snow always reminds me of my past," Persia began as he turned into the same overlook at the river's edge. "My brother. He didn't like to wear his shoes when it snowed. Don't ask me why."

"You have a brother?" From reflections on the water, his face showed surprise. "Mr. Plemons has a son? I didn't know."

"No, he doesn't. I'm adopted." She watched his expression. "You didn't know?"

"No." Jeff hesitated. "Mr. Plemons seldom discusses family."

"Have you ever lost someone you loved?" she asked slightly above a whisper. She felt the warmth of his arms about her. She wanted to connect, express herself, hold nothing back.

"We all do at some point." His expression turned somber. "My mother. I've told you how much I miss her." He ended his statement abruptly and turned to face her. "Where is your brother?"

"Don't know. Have no idea. He was five and I was eight when we lost each other. The sad part is I told him that I'd see that we'd stay together. You see, we were wards of the state of Oklahoma. I promised to take care of the little guy…" A tear erupted, but she secretly wiped it away.

Jeff took her hand. "Why or how did you get separated?"

"Different foster homes. I couldn't help it, Jeff, but still…"

"But you can't blame yourself for something beyond your control," he whispered. "What was his name?"

"Joe Dee Hartsong, and I was Jessie Hartsong. The Plemons had my name changed."

"Changed? Why, for Heaven's sake?" He appeared shocked and stared at her.

"Mumsy, or Mrs. Plemons, had a strange fascination with old Persia. Don't ask me why. She was sorta the artsy type."

"You've shocked me thoroughly. I had no idea. You know what they say, everyone's life is a story. Sounds like yours is no exception."

Persia again felt the warmth of his hand. "Miss Evie's hands were always warm like yours. She was one sweet lady."

"Who?"

"Miss Evie was one of the many foster mothers I had. She was the exception, so sweet. Baked cookies for me daily and read to me… always reading books. I loved her."

"She sounds nice. Guess you don't hear from any of those foster parents, do you?"

"No, but life as a foster child sure makes one grow up fast."

"But look, you turned out okay… wonderful! That's what counts, Persia. We all have some hard knocks along the way." He pushed her hair to the side and rubbed her nose with his.

"I guess. One fact is certain, the Plemons have been great parents to me."

"How long have you lived with them?"

"Since I was twelve. But with Mumsy gone and Bebe sick, I feel kind of uneasy, insecure, I guess you'd say. I can't explain it." She turned toward him. "Am I boring you with all this?"

"No, not at all, but I wouldn't borrow trouble if I were you. At least you have good memories?"

"Of Miss Evie, for sure."

"And she lived in Oklahoma?"

"No, Tennessee. Somewhere near Lebanon, Tennessee."

"In Tennessee? That's a long way from Oklahoma." His eyes widened with surprise.

"I know. Don't ask me how I got there. I can't remember."

"Interesting." He let go of her hand and started the car.

"I've bored you terribly with all this," she whispered. "I guess I needed to talk. Please don't tell anyone, Jeff. I guess Bebe's surgery had its effect on me."

"Is that what you call B. W.? *Bebe*?"

"Yeah, and he's a jewel, too. Just like Mumsy was. I miss her a lot. They took my life and turned it into a Cinderella story. Let's just hope it doesn't end."

"But he's recovering, it seems. Let's hope so."

"Let's do."

Jeff drove slowly into the Shadyside area and stopped at Clairmont.

At the door, he stepped forward and kissed her good night. "I'll call you later," he whispered as he was about to go.

"I'm sorry for pouring out my soul tonight," she said as he let go of her hand. "Please forgive me."

"I have strong shoulders, girl." He tickled her nose. "Don't you worry for a minute."

"Thanks, Jeff. You're sweet."

Upstairs, she kicked off her shoes and flopped across the bed. Sobbing, she cringed at the thought of delving into her tumultuous life while Jeff sat patiently by. "He must have been bored out of his skin. Why should he care?"

"Persia." It was Maud calling from the bottom of the stairs. What did she want at this hour of the night?

"Yes." She got up, wiped her eyes, and hurried to answer.

"Your dad called this evening. He's to get home tomorrow for another doctor's appointment. He's having problems again."

"Oh gosh, should I call him?"

"Don't think I would. He's to arrive home again tomorrow."

"Thanks, Maud. Sounds like bad news. He's sick again."

Chapter 28

"Maud," Persia began at the breakfast table the next morning, "I'm skipping school today. Bebe's sick and I'm worried." Tired from the lack of sleep the night before, she didn't feel like it, anyway. "Did he mention his symptoms?"

"No, made his call very brief," Maud said matter-of-factly.

"Do you reckon it's the cancer again?" Persia asked and nibbled at her food. "Scares me to think about it."

"Now, let's not go worrying before there's reason to—jumping to conclusions. He may have gone back to work too soon. You know what a workaholic he is."

Maud had her way, Like B. W., of sometimes manufacturing bouts of denial. But Persia realized from the housekeeper's expression that she doubted the very words she spoke. Yet, neither debated the issue.

"I wonder what time he's to arrive and how. Should I go to the airport?" Persia asked, still too distraught for food.

"I wouldn't think so. He has all kinds of hired help... the chauffeur will meet the plane, I'm sure. Lloyd knows when and where the boss is at all times," Maud added, referring to B. W.'s long-time help who had taxied him around for ten or more years. "Why don't you go back to bed and get some rest? You look tired."

"Can't. I just toss and turn. I want to see Bebe—greet 'im when he arrives." Tears misted her eyes. She got up from the table to go upstairs. To shower and dress might allay her distress. Too much had happened. Bebe's illness for one, and her silly manner with Jeff the night before, for gosh sakes!

Why had she revealed her past to him? Been so serious. All those silly comments of her childhood and of Joe Dee? He'd courted her as the spoiled, rich daughter of B. W. and Claire Plemons, big oil people, and now he knew better... knew who she really was. She rubbed her brow and undressed. But she liked Jeff. Liked him a lot. If they were ever to have a real relationship, he'd need to know the truth. Trembling, she got into the shower and turned the tap. The warm, almost hot water felt soothing. In just a few hours, Bebe would arrive. Not for a moment could she reveal her concern; that the cancer had returned. She was his main source of strength now that Mumsy was gone, and he was hers. Well, unless he was romantically involved with Sherri Tahlwald. She'd not think about that now.

It was one o'clock that afternoon when Lloyd, the chauffeur, drove the Lexus to the door and stopped. Before she got downstairs, Bebe was already inside.

"Bebe," Persia squealed and ran to hug him. Shocked at his sallow appearance, she knew at once that her fears were true. "You're home.

I stayed home from school to see you. I couldn't wait, Bebe. How do you feel?"

He kissed her cheek. "Got to get back with my doctor. I don't feel well at all. Can't shake this thing, sweetie."

"I'm sorry. What hurts, Bebe?"

"What doesn't?" He smiled wearily. "I'm weak, honey, and my appetite has gone—completely gone."

Maud stood aside watching. "Why don't I heat some chicken soup? You know what they say. It cures everything." She smiled.

"Just give me a few minutes, Maud. But thanks. It's great to get home," he replied and glanced about for a chair.

"I hope you're here to stay," Persia interjected. "I want you here, Bebe." She took his hand and led him to the family room. "Do I need to call Dr. Levy for an appointment?"

"I called from down there... made sure I got in to see him soon. My appointment's at ten tomorrow."

"Look, Bebe, I plan to stay home tomorrow and drive you in." She again noticed his weary, ashen face. He must have lost at least twenty pounds.

"No, dear, that's not necessary. I told Lloyd to pick me up. I knew you'd be in school."

"But, Bebe, how often have I done favors for you? You've been away."

"But, dear, it'll probably take most of the day—tests. You realize they take time." An embarrassed expression showed in his soulful eyes... regret for staying away so long.

"I can wait. Don't mind at all. They have magazines to read, and I can always go for a Coke."

"Sweetie, I suspect this is nothing. I probably didn't take proper care after my surgery. Please go on to school. I'll give you a full account tomorrow evening, and I do plan to spend the holidays here if that's any consolation." He managed to grin.

So it was. The next morning, Persia jumped out of bed, showered, and bounced downstairs to the kitchen for a glass of orange juice before leaving for school. In no mood for food, she gulped down the juice and mumbled "good morning" to Maud. Strangely, Maud didn't respond. She'd already spilled juice on the kitchen counter and sworn at the toaster when the toast didn't pop up fast enough.

Persia pretended not to notice and got up to leave. "You call me at school, Maud, if Bebe gets home before I do." She jotted a number. Maud took it but made no comment, obviously worried that the boss was beyond anything that medical experts could do.

All day, Persia tried desperately to concentrate. More than once during class, her thoughts wandered. Whatever Professor Downey said didn't really matter. She'd not stay for her sorority meeting afterwards, either.

"Maud," she said on the telephone later. "Is Bebe home yet?" She gasped into the telephone.

"Got here about one." Maud didn't elaborate.

"What was his problem? What did Dr. Levy say?"

"Your dad's asleep, hon. I think he needs rest. The doctor gave him something to make him relax." She hesitated. "Lloyd helped me to set up a hospital bed in the library. I'm letting him rest."

"He didn't tell you anything? What the doctor said?"

"No, and I didn't ask. Thought he'd tell us later."

At home that evening, Persia threw her backpack down and tiptoed into the library. Surprisingly, B. W. lay staring at the ceiling. "Bebe," she whispered and patted his arm. "How do you feel?"

"They did an MRI, didn't comment much," he gasped between breaths. "He did some blood work, too. Said he'd let me know more in a few days."

"But you're so pale. Are you hungry?"

"Not now. Maud will heat some soup later, I guess. I'm tired mostly. How was school?"

"Okay, I guess."

"How much longer in the semester?"

Persia stared at him, puzzled. Why did it matter, such a big deal? "Some over two weeks. Finals the first week in December."

"You stay focused now. Don't let me distract you. You've put a lot of work into your classes. Make the best of it."

"I will, Bebe, but I can't help but worry. I love you, and you're sick," she sobbed. "Please get well. I'd be lost without you." She squeezed his hand as she looked into his face.

He closed his eyes, and she tiptoed out. They'd visit later.

Thanksgiving came and went with only a couple of high points as far as Persia was concerned. Bebe was able to take his place at the Thanksgiving table, though his eating was sparse, and Molly was in town. Too bad Molly couldn't join them for dinner; Maud had outdone herself with the turkey and trimmings. Lloyd came. His wife had died two months previously, and Bebe suggested he be invited. The conversation was pleasant, upbeat, and if B. W. noticed Claire's empty place at the table, he didn't comment. Could be he wanted to avoid the darker moments and dwell on the positive. After the meal, he and Lloyd enjoyed the first half of a ballgame before B. W. excused himself to take a pain pill.

Later, Persia squealed when Molly called. "When can I see you?" she asked her former high school friend.

"Why don't we meet tomorrow for lunch. Haven't seen you in ages," Molly insisted in her upbeat way.

Persia hesitated. Should she leave Bebe? But he insisted that she go on with her life. "Lunch? Where?" she finally said.

"Margello's on the Strip. Sound okay? We need to touch base, laugh a little. I'm dying to see you."

"Sounds good."

"How in the world are you?" Persia gasped when she saw her friend… still petite and pretty, with enough giggles for six.

"Glad to be home and get some rest," Molly replied and gave Persia a hug. "So nice to see you."

"You, too. I miss our gab sessions, besides all our foolishness," Persia giggled as they found a booth near the back. "Wasn't high school fun?"

The chitchat continued over a broad spectrum; obviously, Molly wanted to hear of Persia's school activities. Were her classes hard? Did her professors give pop quizzes? And did many of them speak with an accent? "It's crazy," Molly said. "I can't understand a word they say." She smiled. "Oh, by the way, are you seeing much of Jeff?"

"Off and on, mostly off," Persia smirked and rolled her eyes. "I guess he likes to keep me guessing."

"Could be busy. Does he work?"

"He takes law classes, he says, and yeah, he has a full time job."

"See, that might just be the case… busy."

"If you want to hypothesize," Persia cracked with a giggle. "You haven't changed, Molly. So what's it with you? Any Romeos at your school?"

"Oh, if so, I haven't found them. I guess I don't have that seductive lure about me." She laughed. "Say, speakin' of Jeff, did you ever tell him the full story of the spring break ordeal?"

"You mean the attack? You knew that he came down in my dad's company plane to escort me home?"

"I meant the drink incident, that guy that kept following you around."

"Heavens, no. He'd think me crazy for sure… the biggest airhead in the country. I hope I've grown up since then." Persia looked away.

"But we did have fun otherwise; something to tell your future kids, I guess," Molly said.

"If we have any. At this point, I wonder." They both giggled.

They ordered and giggled at past incidents of times gone by. "Gonna do anything big for Christmas?" Molly asked as they began the meal.

"Not me. Jeff might call. Your guess is as good as mine," Persia said, feeling sad. Should she mention Bebe's illness? On second thought, she wouldn't. Why spoil a nice day? And Molly expected to find her happy, kidding around and full of laughs. "And you? You'll come home, won't you?"

"No, I have a part-time job at school. I need the money."

"A job? At what?"

"The university library remains open over the holidays, and I'm to work at the checkout desk. Can't get any easier than that."

"Guess we'll have to look forward to summer," Persia said with a faraway stare.

"Probably. I'd really like to go abroad, if I had the funds, but guess it's out for now. Not while I'm in school."

Summer? Something about the word stung like a bee had popped her. If Bebe's cancer had spread, would he even be around by summer? "Yeah," she mumbled, not really aware of what she'd uttered. Suddenly, she felt dizzy!

"Are you all right?" Molly asked as she stared across the table. "Is it Jeff you're worried about?"

"I'm okay, just rushed." She pushed her plate aside. "I have to go, Molly."

"Go?"

"I have to help Maud with the chores." She hurriedly took two ten-dollar bills from her wallet and laid them on the table.

"You didn't tell me," Molly blurted, obviously surprised. "And look, put your money away. I meant to treat you."

"Thanks, Molly, but it's on me. We'll talk later. Okay?"

"Take care," Molly stammered as she watched her friend rush away.

Outside, Persia frantically started the car to head home. What had come over her? she wondered, already embarrassed. A panic attack? She pressed the accelerator and zoomed out of the parking lot. Bebe's ill. I can't bear to think of it. I just know he's gonna die.

CHAPTER 29

"PERSIA, DO YOU HAVE a minute?" B. W. called from his hospital bed in the library. She and Maud were busy hanging a Christmas wreath above the fireplace, one of the only decorations they planned to display. With B. W. ill, no one was in a holiday spirit.

"Be right there," she replied and hurried to see what he needed.

"Drag up a chair. We need to talk," he said in a subdued voice. His somber face showed signs of strain and was more ashen than usual. His mahogany-colored hair fell across his brow.

The semester at school had ended and exams past. The mid-December weather was cold and the pre-holiday season already in progress; the upscale neighborhood of Shadyside was adorned with all kinds of decorations. Everyone seemed ready for the holidays... well, everyone except the Plemonses.

"I haven't told you, sweetie, but Dr. Levy says that my condition is worse—pancreatic cancer. He says the disease has spread and there's not much else he can do. It doesn't look good, dear, and you—"

"Bebe, it can't be." She stood, stunned, tears erupting like rain. "You mean? You didn't tell me."

"But you had exams to pass. Guess it's time to tell you that I may not be long for this world." Tears filled his eyes. "We need to talk business for a while... company business. You're my only heir."

Persia flung herself over him, sobbing. "You can't, Bebe. You can't leave me. I don't care about money."

Neither spoke for a moment, merely sobbed. "I so hoped you'd recover," she finally muttered between sobs. "What will I ever do without you—and Mumsy's gone, too."

"But I have to prepare you for the future. It's in your best interest and the company's." He's gained composure and spoke in a businesslike manner.

"Oh, Bebe, please don't say it. I don't care about Wesco or—"

"But after I'm gone, you will. You'll learn to go on with your life. A brighter day will dawn and you'll need something to fall back on. I'm to leave fifty percent of Wesco holdings to you."

"But, Bebe, I don't know anything about the company, the management of it. Do you mean I'd run that place? I want a family, a mother and a father, the way we used to be. Do you realize I'll be all alone?"

He drew her to him as she rested her head on his chest. "I can't control fate, baby, but I can see to it that you never go hungry, want for anything, and I intend to." He wiped tears from his face with his hand. "You've given Claire and me so much happiness in the short time that we were a family." Again, he wiped his face. "Claire's eyes never glistened so brightly as when she first saw you. She referred to you as her angel. Remember how she loved the finer things—art, classical music, and such? With her, you fit right into that category, all things beautiful." He managed to grin.

Persia leaned against him, silently sobbing but wanting to hear every utterance he made. Seldom had she seen him weep, except at the loss of his wife, and it'd been seldom that he'd spoken so endearingly.

"She'd often tell me that you were a living work of art—perfection," he added. "I guess that's how the name *Persia* came about."

"Really? I wondered, but didn't want to hurt her feelings."

"Some lofty ideas she had regarding the old country and culture. All the ancient glory."

"She's gone, Bebe, and now it's you. Where does that leave me?"

"You know I'd never leave you if I could control my destiny." He patted her shoulder. "But the Wesco stock will be there for you. I can arrange that much, and that's what I intend to do."

"Stock?"

"I've decided to go public with the company, list it on the stock market. Elliot Romble is to become the new CEO. He'll manage the IPO, but because you'll own much of the stock, I do hope you'll stay abreast of transactions." He patted her shoulder again. "Can I count on it... carry on the Plemons name?"

Persia hesitated before she answered. *I'll remain Persia Plemons instead of Jessie Hartsong, he's asking. With both of them gone, why couldn't I take my old name back? But he did have a point. What chance in the world do I have of connecting with my biological family?* "Sure, Bebe. You've shown great generosity. Of course, I will. Do you think all this would have Mumsy's approval?"

"Of course. Claire wanted the best for you. She was a wonderful partner in business *and* in life."

"Is Sherri anything like Mumsy, Bebe? I've wondered. You've never discussed her much." She noticed his expression changed. "Did I speak out of turn?"

"No, no one ever will come up to Claire... never will." He moved slightly and wiped his face again. "Speaking of Sherri, we're not together anymore."

"You mean, oh, Bebe. Was I to blame? It was just..."

"No, not at all. After I got sick, I guess she lost interest. Quit coming around, and well, in fact, she went on alone on the cruise to Norway."

"I'm sorry I acted ugly toward her." Persia tucked her chin. "She wasn't Mumsy. She had an aloof way about her, too, like I was extra or a spare tire, I guess I could say. I just wanted you to myself. Can you ever forgive me?"

"I knew that. I knew all those things you were feeling, but I was lonely dear. When you lose someone tied to your heart, it hurts, hurts bad." Tears arose and burst down his face.

"Like I am about my brother. I'll never see him again. I'm sure of it, Bebe. My heart aches for him, too. We were close. As children, I took care of the little guy when Mama would leave for work."

B. W. reached for her.

"You and Mumsy made life fun again," she said and smiled.

"And you helped us. You brought sunshine to us as well."

"When you're gone—" She didn't finish but sat sobbing, then bent and kissed his cheek.

"You'll see the glow of sunrise again, baby, the rosy glow of a new day. You're beautiful and so capable of love. Those who need love, know best how to give it. You remember what I say—give love and it comes back to you." He lifted his head and looked toward a nearby table. "See that little velvet case over there? Would you hand it to me, please?

Persia saw it and handed it to him, then watched as he gently opened it.

"I bought this diamond necklace for Claire as a celebration gift when we adopted you. He held up an expensive, at least three carat, diamond necklace. "I want you to have it."

"It's beautiful, Bebe." A tear burst from her eyes. "It's gorgeous. You bought it?"

"When you wear it, you'll know that our love is with you still. Will you remember?"

"Of course, Bebe. But I'd remember anyway. How could I ever forget? She gave him a kiss and laid the necklace aside.

* * * * * * * * * * * *

It was a sad day a week later that B. W. peacefully passed away while Persia sat holding his hand. They spent the previous week unraveling business details and his personal wishes as to Clairmont (she could continue in the spacious dwelling or sell it) and other personal objects of art and furniture.

Now that he was gone, it fell to her to see that proper respect was shown. She submitted a brief obituary to the local paper and issued a press release to outgoing media. A memorial service occurred two days later at the Chapel of the Angels, which drew a crowd totally beyond her imagination. Business associates flew in from across the country to express respect for a man they described as decent and honest, "a tower of honor," as one gentleman put it.

After the crowd dispersed, only she and Maud accompanied Pastor Evanston to the cemetery for a private graveside prayer. There in the old cemetery adjoining the Chapel, with an occasional snowflake drifting down onto the freshly prepared grave, Persia listened to a simple plea to God for a good man's soul. She thought of all Bebe had meant to her: a father when she had none, a provider when she was poor, and an advisor who saw to it that she'd have a secure future.

The day ended stressfully and sad. Back home at Clairmont, she and Maud closed the door to the library, unable to disassemble the hospital bed, and moped about the house like two lost puppies.

* * *   * * *   * * *

As the next few days passed, Maud spoke less and less. B. W. had been her idol, her boss, her security. She lived to please the man whom she trusted and admired. Her sorrow was obvious.

"Are you well, Maud?" Persia asked one morning at breakfast.

"I'm okay. Guess I should be looking at the want ads."

"Want ads? You're about to leave me? Don't tell me that you're considering a move."

"But you won't keep this old house. You're young. You've got your whole life ahead."

"I plan to stay here until spring. I need time to think." She sipped her juice in deep thought. "We shouldn't make important decisions in haste. Haven't you heard that from experts?"

Maud's face brightened. "It's a deal, child. We'll stay here and console each other. I need someone and so do you."

Persia stepped to the housekeeper and gave her a hug. "You're a part of this place, Maud. Don't you worry for a moment about a job. Bebe would want me to take care of you."

Maud wiped tears from her eyes and stepped to the desk in the family room. "You have some letters in here. Did you see them?"

"Letters? Me?" Persia went to check. "Probably sympathy cards. I've received tons of them lately." She picked one up. "Hmmm. South Carolina," she mumbled and tore the envelope open. "Reid Morgan. My word, I never did answer his last note." She quickly scanned the note and smiled. "He wants me to go see him this Christmas weekend."

"Who?" Maud inquired and rubbed her hands on her apron.

"A guy I met in South Carolina, a scientist."

"You're going, aren't you?" Maud said emphatically. "It'd do you good."

"I can't now. I'm supposed to go back to Oklahoma City for another checkup with Dr. Brody… the head injury, you remember. But I sure will go in the spring. Reid is one smart man."

"I think you should," Maud said. "You go to South Carolina, and I'll go to Missouri to visit my brother. Okay?"

"You go on, Maud. I can't go to see Reid now. I'll see Reid in the spring. I want to."

She picked up the other letter and tore the envelope open. "Jeff" written at the bottom caught her eye.

"I've meant to tell you for some time now, but I knew you had a lot to deal with. Remember I told you that a young woman whom I dated flew off to Italy to attend a culinary school? She's home. She decided that she missed me. We're to marry in February."

Dumbfounded and crushed, Persia stomped out and down the stairs. "He didn't even have the guts to tell me to my face!" Yep, she'd leave for Oklahoma on the earliest plane out. Surely, there was something interesting out there somewhere.

CHAPTER 30

JOE PICKED UP ONE of the boots Claudia gave him for Christmas and wiped the dust off it with a tissue. She had followed High Pockets east to make sure her prize horse got the best care possible while he and Dan, her new trainer, worked to diagnose the colt's hang-ups. If ever High pockets was to show racing ability it was time, she'd said. "See what you can do and here's a little token of appreciation that might lift your spirits in the meantime… a pair of riding boots and a handsome set of aqua-blue silks. As you know, Joe, blue is our color at Whispering Trails. You make a winner outta my horse and you can wear them often." Her eyes, bright as ever, danced with enthusiasm. One perky lady, he thought, as he remembered her charm.

"Just like Claudia," Joe commented to Dan after she left. "She's one jewel of a lady, but her horse—well, we'll see. He seems to have developed some problems since I worked with 'im in California."

Dan shook his head in his usual manner and listened. "Our work may be cut out for us. Horses have a mindset of their own, I've found. Something could've happened to 'im, health problems maybe."

With the November meet past and a new year ahead, Joe felt pressured to do what he could with High Pockets, under Dan's guidance, of course. He liked Dan, a short man with a middle bulge and a lot of tousled hair, and a face that denoted confidence; not a hint of haughtiness in it. Easy to talk to—real nice guy, Joe decided and told himself that Claudia had demonstrated skill in securing Dan. Surely, if anyone could determine High Pocket's abilities, he could.

"If my horse can run," Claudia had stated in desperation, "get it out of 'im. If he can't, or won't, I'll put 'im out to stud." She grimaced in her stubborn manner and flitted away.

Joe remembered, too, how Chub, her former trainer had said, "The best of pedigrees doesn't necessarily guarantee success." Now to think that Claudia had put her horse's future in his hands thrilled him to no end, and the boots? Whether he'd ever wear them in a major race was doubtful. He'd polished them weekly since Christmas and modeled the silks more than once. To don the pretty blue and gold outfit never failed to buoy his spirits—build confidence. When time permitted, he usually went to the grandstand to eat and mingle with the crowd. Not yet eighteen, he was legally prohibited from placing bets, but while rambling about, it wasn't unusual to run upon a racetrack novice who was willing to take his advice regarding bet choices, which boosted his ego even more. Churchill Downs was like Heaven, and if he did nothing more than exist there, he felt he'd found his dream.

* * * \ * * * \ * * *

Mid-January weather in Louisville was cold except for a few sunny days that pumped new energy into Joe—gave him an urgency to jump out of bed, dress, and get High Pockets out for an early morning gallop. Breakfast came later, usually with Dan. They'd discuss the horse and any obvious changes in the colt's behavior, as Claudia requested. "Find out what makes that horse run, or balk if that be the case," she'd said, and Joe had noticed a reluctance in High Pockets, which Chub termed a "closer." "Some horses are front runners," he'd said, "and some are closers. Closers start slow and warm to the race." Whether Chub had it right was, again, anyone's guess.

"What kind of trainer was he—Chub?" Dan asked one morning at breakfast.

"Good, knew a lot about horses." Joe thought for a minute. "Strict, though... very. Chewed me out more than once, but I guess I deserved it." He grinned in his boyish manner.

"Do you reckon he was too strict... too forceful? A horse can sense when he's made to perform," Dan added. "He'll balk every time."

"That horse used to run like crazy, but since she brought 'im here, I've noticed a difference. He'll go about forty feet with me and stop—crazier than the devil."

"We need to look into that. It'll never do in racing. I think I'll have the vet take a look at 'im; make sure he's physically okay," Dan added. "He could have a leg problem."

"Might not hurt."

"I've been thinking," Dan commented. "The hay here may not agree with 'im... not likely, but could be a factor, or the weather. Horses are sometimes sensitive to minor changes, the slightest factors."

"Hadn't thought of it like that. Everything's new to 'im here," Joe agreed. "That's for sure."

"The next time he balks on you, just stop and lead 'im back to the barn. Don't force. Let's give 'im some slack," Dan instructed before he left for a meeting. "Work 'im easy and see what happens."

* * * *   * * * *   * * * *

Joe jumped out of bed the next morning eager to try the horse again. Dan's idea sounded reasonable. Surely the pretty horse had the right physical features—sixteen hands tall, bright eyes and coat, long legs, and strong build. Joe put the saddle on, fastened the girth beneath the belly, and pulled himself into the saddle. With a slight whack on the rear, he felt High Pockets's strong muscles contract into a dash forward... full stride. "Maybe this boy will run this morning," he mumbled, and tightened the grip on the reins. "Good boy," he coaxed. "Let's go." High Pockets sprinted forward and was at the first turn of the track before Joe sensed any change in stride at all. Another slight whack and High Pockets went faster. "Good boy," Joe whispered as he leaned forward to prod the horse forward.

The run was better than usual; High Pockets appeared to give it his all except at the very last when he began to switch his tail in protest. Joe knew that meant rebellion. He pulled the reins and jumped off to lead the colt back to the barn as Dan instructed. "Work 'im easy; make 'im think he's the boss," Joe reminded himself of Dan's advice.

Back in the barn, Joe was about to put High Pockets in his stall when Rick Stubblefield came whistling around the corner. His face shone like a new BMW. "Wanna gallop Gravi Train one last time?" Rick said. "He's to leave for New Mexico tomorrow."

"Sure. High Pockets here didn't run full time. I can spare a few minutes," Joe mumbled, already miffed. He'd worked with Rick for months, but Rick pulled a fast one and contracted Tony Ingles to ride Gravi. What the heck? he told himself. Why sweat it? One more disappointment wouldn't kill 'im. Not after what he'd lived through. "Sure, I'll run 'im."

"The Sunday edition of the paper out in New Mexico sure gave Gravi a build-up yesterday," Rick bragged, obviously thrilled. "The horse is the one to beat," it stated. "Sure causing a stir… great expectations."

"Guess Mr. Murdock back in Bristow is up in the clouds with that. You going, too?" Joe noticed Rick didn't make eye contact. Guess he knows he let me down, Joe thought, still miffed.

"Oh, sure. Wouldn't miss it," Rick beamed. "Gotta see my horse come in."

"Let's hope he does," Joe grunted as he got on Gravi and galloped off. "Let's hope he does."

By the time the gallop with Gravi ended. Dan had arrived and motioned for Joe to meet him in his office. Joe led the colt to the stall and rubbed his palm across the horse's nose. "See ya, boy. Do a good job for 'em tomorrow. Show your stuff. Okay, boy?" Joe turned to go to see what Dan wanted.

"Sit down a minute," Dan said. "Had a call from Claudia."

Joe sat across from him and stared into his face. "Claudia?"

"Yeah, she wanted to know about High Pockets's progress, and guess what?"

Joe's eyes widened. Had Claudia decided to sell her horse? "What?" he blurted impatiently.

"She wants us to take the horse to Oaklawn as a pretrial for the Derby. Stunned, Joe jumped from his chair. "You gotta be kiddin'."

"And guess what else? You're to be in the irons—ride that son of a gun."

Joe almost choked; his heart tumbled. "Me?"

"She thinks—and she does have a point—it'd be good for 'im to learn to compete, experience, with the big boys," Dan explained.

Joe thought for a moment. "High Pockets has improved, but Oaklawn? Some of the best racin' in the country is at Oaklawn. When?" He frowned nervously.

"Some time in February. I'll have to arrange a date and check with them," Dan said and scratched his head. "See what's available."

"To see me be embarrassed, yeah, Dan. I'm not so sure what that horse will do. He might git out there and lie down." Joe managed to chuckle. "I know one thing. I got my work cut out for me. Sure as heck do. Kind of like walking through fire, too."

"It'll be good experience for you and the horse. Besides, you know the horse better'n anybody," Dan consoled. "Why hire a stranger to ride 'im? That's Claudia's feeling and she's right. What does she have to lose? Either her horse will come through or fail," Dan said with his jaw squared. "She's right about this one."

* * * *   * * * *   * * * *

January slid into February, and Joe hardly noticed the change; he'd worked long days with High Pockets with hardly breathing time to spare. His racing schedule at Oaklawn was set for the 21st, a mere three weeks away, and to say that his mental state was ready certainly defied truth—he'd never felt so edgy in his life.

Would his first try at a major race end as a bummer? As he stepped to the stable to saddle High Pockets for his morning workout, Rick Stubblefield happened up, this time his face sullen and glum. "You all right?" Joe asked, concerned. Why did he bother to ask, he wondered. Rick had demonstrated no regard for him in hiring Tony Ingles as jockey for the New Mexico race. Good enough for 'im that the jockey disappointed 'im, Joe thought, if that be the case.

"Lost. Gravi didn't so much as show." Rick's expression dropped even more as he shook his head in exasperation. He pursed his lips with a furrowed brow.

"You're kiddin'," Joe responded. "What happened?"

"Ingles couldn't get it out of 'im… the colt balked something fierce, lost time from the beginning. Finally did get to the finish line, but behind… way behind. I couldn't stand to watch it."

"Too bad," Joe mumbled and turned to go. He wouldn't say, "I told you so," but he wanted to. Maybe Rick had learned a lesson. But he'd not rub it in… too much else to worry about. Oaklawn in February… my gosh, how he dreaded it.

CHAPTER 31

CHRISTMAS, AND GOSH, HOW lonely! To think a new year about to begin and here I sit alone, Persia reflected in the family room at Claremont. Mumsy gone—Bebe, too, even Maud gone to visit her brother in Missouri. And to think another trip to Oklahoma for a final check with Dr. Brody. Not that another visit to him would be so bad, but a doctor's appointment at Christmas? Not the most exciting way to spend the holidays.

Getting up from her chair, she ambled into the kitchen where so much reminded her of her parents; their favorite chairs, Bebe's especially, where he sat to read the morning paper, and the elaborate coffeepot where he brewed the morning coffee. Not hungry, she turned to pace the long corridor down to the library. To muster the courage to go it alone scared her terribly. And the business of disposing of the mansion—how could she ever care for such a vast estate? The mere thought gave her chills. And there was Mumsy's expensive art collection, furnishings and personals. The tightness in her chest, which she'd experienced so often of late, returned. Actually she didn't want the big house—the responsibility of such treasures and upkeep. Claremont was Mumsy's idea, not hers. Guess there is a bright side to all this somewhere; to fret over it all did take her mind off Jeff... the idiot! In February, mere weeks away, he'd wed his old flame, whatever her name was. Why hadn't she seen it coming—all the absenteeism, promises to see her and failing to show up? She swiped her hair to the side nervously. I'd like to wring his neck!

* * * * * * * * *

Christmas passed without the usual social whirl. Even Molly had decided to remain at school to take a part-time job. "I need the money," she said when Persia insisted she come home for the holidays. As it happened, the holiday break proved better than expected. She'd busied herself with dozens of thank you notes for the many condolences at Bebe's passing, tearing up with each one. A note of apology to Molly, too. "I'm sorry for my behavior the day we met for lunch," she scribbled, to which Molly, in her thoughtful manner responded, "Why in Heaven's name didn't you let me in on your father's condition? Don't you realize that's what friends are for?" Just like Molly, Persia mused, again wiping tears. "She's one in a million. If I ever get married, she'll be my maid of honor. Married? Oh gosh, married? Can't say I'll ever trust another man, not after the way Jeff did me.

She *had* sent Reid Morgan a note. "I've had illness and death in my family, but expect me in the spring when school is out. I promise I'll see you then."

**** **** ****

The flight to Oklahoma City was pleasant; a change definitely from the ho-hum of Claremont. At Will Rogers Airport, she grabbed her bag at Baggage Claim and hurried to Avis Rent A Car. She'd need transportation, especially for the drive south to Wesco, if she decided to visit the place. Bebe had requested she do so. "You need to acquaint yourself with the business, honey," he'd said a few days before his passing. And she had nothing better to do after her appointment with Dr. Brody at ten.

Getting into the Ford Focus, she glanced about, happy to see the city again—those smiling Oklahoma faces, she thought gleefully. No place in the world like it. Her spirits soared. Yep, Oklahoma again. Some of the best people in the world; their twangy voices, accommodating manner, and all that enthusiasm for sports... felt like home again! Home? She barely remembered her Oklahoma home at Carlisle with Joe Dee and Mama, but to say the least, she knew she'd been born in Oklahoma. Even started to school at Lawton Elementary. My gosh, that all seems eons ago. Wonder if Mama still lives at Carlisle. And Joe Dee, the kid must be fifteen or more by now. She rushed into the Sheridan to check in.

At the doctor's office, she entered, checked in at the front desk, and took a chair beside a small table with magazines. Little about the place had changed since her last visit. Taking a magazine, she opened it to see an article on Philbrook Museum in Tulsa. They had just ended their annual Festival of Trees event. One fact she read was on the good art collection the museum owned—a result of old oil money, she reasoned. Quite possibly, Claremont might turn out the same. Philbrook was once a residence, owned by oil people, too—people who came from the East like Bebe and his dad, who first started in the coal business and had later come to Oklahoma when oil hit it big.

"Good morning, Miss Plemons," the nurse greeted. "Dr. Brody is ready to see you."

Persia followed her into an examining room and took a seat to wait.

"He'll be right with you," the nurse said and, with a comforting smile, left.

The door soon opened, and Dr. Brody's face broke into the broadest grin ever. "How are you, Miss Plemons? Nice to see you again." He stood before her, erect and perfectly groomed. His eyes beamed with enthusiasm as they began the usual, "doctor visit" conversation—"How have you felt? Are you experiencing pain of any sort?"

"Sad is all. My dad passed away recently." Her voice cracked as she almost lost her composure.

"I heard about his passing. He'll certainly be missed here. He was very kind to our city, sponsored many charities, sure a super person. I met him once at the Rotary Club and was very impressed."

"Thanks," she whispered, her eyes misting at the mention of Bebe's name. "I sure miss him."

"But tell me. Have you experienced any unusual pain or sensation?" Dr. Brody appeared ready to get down to business.

"None to speak of. Stress is all, and I think I told you last time that my memory is back... just as you said it'd do. I was driving down the highway here, and suddenly everything came back clear as glass." She glanced up at him to see his gorgeous blue eyes studying hers. "I can remember my childhood as though it was yesterday."

"I think you did tell me earlier, and I'm elated that it all happened as we thought it would. Recovery is always good news. So now you're back to normal."

"Yes, I've graduated from high school and already finished one semester of college."

"And you've come back to visit us here. Did you tell me you were born here?"

"At Carlisle. Ever hear of it? Out of Lawton some few miles."

"Can't say that I have. I grew up in Ponca City, but went to Nashville to medical school. You see, I've lived all over until recently when I moved here to practice." He smiled and stepped back to check the scar where the injury was. "No problem. Looks like a complete heal."

"That's good to hear. I guess I had a narrow escape—with death, that is."

"So how long do you plan to be in town?" he asked, as though anxious to move on.

Surprised that he'd ask, she blurted, "A couple of days is all. My second semester at school begins January 10th. She noticed he didn't wear a wedding band.

They chatted a few more minutes about Oklahoma's basketball team, her school activities, and future plans before he finally said, "I guess we can dismiss you then." He grinned. "But look, don't forget us. Don't stay away too long." He extended a hand to hers with another broad grin before saying goodbye.

Alone again in the examining room, she prepared to leave. Dr. Brody had certainly made her feel better. He was handsome and interesting, but would she ever see him again? With no future appointments, probably not, a shame, darn it. Just like Jeff, nothing seemed to gel. Jeff? Not again. Why did so many little instances remind her all over again? A pang of anger surged over her. I hate 'im, hate 'im, totally hate 'im. She reached the car and got in. "I hope I never lay eyes on 'im again," she kept mumbling and started the motor. "I hate 'im."

Something about the visit with Dr. Brody affected her like an elixir, gave her new zest, a desire to explore; chat and visit the place. Whizzing the car around, she headed downtown; the Capital, the Ford Center, the Cowboy Hall of Fame. If time permitted, she wanted to see them all. But lunch? Would she eat in town or find a small restaurant out somewhere? The latter struck her as interesting.

Turning west, she found the intersection of Interstate 40 and H. E. Bailey Turnpike. Heading south, the road rose up to meet her like welcoming arms of family! Lawton, why not drive down; see how the place had changed. Time takes its toll, she told herself. Ten years was a long time. A sign to Chickasha appeared and soon disappeared. Had Mama remarried, changed her name from Hartsong? Had she moved away, clear out of the state? Hunger gave way to curiosity. "I'm going to Carlisle," she mumbled, desperate to revisit the place. "There's no better time. I'm going to find Mama, and I might as well prepare for a shock."

At Lawton, she turned right off the highway, then soon right again onto a narrow winding road that led northwest. Surprised at the changes in the area, she hardly recognized it. New houses, small businesses, and churches of all faiths dotted the roadside. Soon, the narrow road widened into a four-lane highway. Trailer courts? Oh, darn, what was the name of our place back then? At a nearby service station, she pulled over to ask.

"No trailer courts here, ma'am," the attendant said flippantly and went about his business. "A few trailers over on the east side, but no courts."

"None?" Persia tried not to show her disaapointment.

"Not to my knowledge. Carlisle has tripled in population in recent times. You might ask around."

"Thanks," she mumbled, disappointed.

Already disturbed, she left, not willing to give up. *That guy can't be more than thirty; how would he know the history of this place—not unless he grew up here?* Turning to drive farther into the business district... a Target, Super Drugs, Auto Parts, at least ten businesses stood strung along Main Street, but soon the businesses ended—only residences with neatly trimmed lawns. At the sight of a sixtyish-looking man mowing, she pulled over.

"Sir, are there any trailer courts in Carlisle? I'm looking for a relative," she explained in her most polite manner.

He stopped the mower and yelled. "Didn't hear. Whatcha say?"

"I'm looking for a trailer court that used to be here in Carlisle. Had trees around and a brook to one side. Are you familiar with anything such as that?"

He scratched his head as if in deep thought. "How long ago, ma'am?"

"At least ten years."

"I'll bet you're thinking of old Shadybrook." He frowned. "That court was demolished some time ago. They've cleaned the site for our new mega-mart... building supplies."

"Cleared it?" Stunned, she stared in disbelief.

"Oh, yes, ma'am. It got kinda rough out there, a lot of drug-dealing and drunks, I guess you could say. We was mighty glad to see it go."

Oh gosh, had Mama become addicted to drugs... alcohol was bad enough. So all those trailers over there were moved or destroyed?"

"A few moved to the east side over by the ball field, but none to speak of." He appeared eager to get on with his mowing.

"Thanks," she muttered, confused.

East side over by the ball field. Why not drive by and take a look? It was on her way out, anyway.

Approximately a half mile beyond the business district, she saw three trailers situated in a row and facing the narrow street. The first appeared new, quite messy, with toys on the lawn. The second, not much better. The third showed age, weathered, but flowerbeds filled with bright colored flowers struck her as a place of an older person, a lady perhaps—the flowers. She pulled into the driveway and knocked on the door. An elderly woman, stooped and pale, answered.

"Ma'am," Persia began. "I'm looking for the Shadybrook Trailer Court that used to be in Carlisle. They tell me it's gone, but did you know any of the residents?" She observed the old woman's face. Her dark eyes shown like gems embedded in molten rock. Her jowls drooped to form small pouches at the corners of her mouth.

"Yes, ma'am, it's gone. Done away with some time ago. See them bulldozers there? That's where a new business is going in." She pointed. "Me and these two others here are all that's left."

"But the trees and the little brook that my brother used to wade in—it's gone, too."

"Yep, that man that bought the site come down from Chicago and cleared up this entire area. Sure changed things around if you ask me." Her brow knitted into a snarl.

"You've lived at the Shadybrook, I assume?"

"Sure did, right up to the end. Then had to hire a man to move me here."

Persia straightened her stance and looked the old woman straight in the eye. "Did you ever know a family by the name of *Hartsong*?"

The woman sighed, then said, "Knew a Hartsong woman, let's see. Her name was Rebecca—went by Becky, best I remember. Had two children that she was always mentioning."

Persia gasped. "You sure of that? What happened to her? Did she move?"

"She died a few years back, with cancer. Heavy smoker, she was." The woman paused. "Won't you come in, Miss, have a glass of cold lemonade?"

Persia stepped up on the single doorstep and on into the dwelling. "I'm Jessie, her daughter."

"My goodness! You don't say. What she would've given to see you, child! My name is Ida Studebaker. Your mama sure did love you. Talked about you constantly, especially after she got sick. Always hoped she'd see you again."

"I have a brother, too. Not sure where he is. We lost touch a long time ago. Did she ever mention where he might be?" Persia watched the woman's face, anxious for her answer.

An emphatic look broke across the stranger's face. "No, she always wondered herself. Felt like she'd let her kids down, as she always put it. I felt real sorry for her... real sorry for her."

"Did my mother suffer much—with the cancer?"

"Wasn't easy at all. The treatments mostly. I'm so sorry you missed her. She was a pitiful case."

"You see, Ida—may I call you Ida? I was adopted and they changed my name to Persia… Persia Plemons of Wesco Oil. Ever hear of it?"

"I guess so. I'm not much on the businesses around here. You say they changed your name? Didn't you put up a stink?" She grinned, then frowned.

"Oh, no. I was so happy to get parents, real parents, that I didn't care what they called me." Persia glanced away as memories of Bebe and Mumsy came to mind. "They were super parents, too." She sighed. "But they're both dead now, too."

Ida's facial expression turned somber.

"But tell me, did Mama mention why she let us go—to the state, you know, gave us up?"

"Just said she was unable to provide for you. She hated the idea, too. Cried often when she spoke of you. You know, I don't think it hurt her—the cancer—any more than giving up her kids."

Tears rose in Persia's eyes. "No more than I wanted to return to her. And poor little Joe Dee cried for weeks, wanting to go home to Mama." She wiped the tears from her face. "Do you know where Mama is buried? Her gravesite?"

"No, have no idea, hon. She did speak on occasion of her deceased husband. Wherever he rests, I guess is where she is, too. Would be my guess."

"Ida, you've brought sad news, yes, but yet happy news, too, if you know what I mean… closure. I wanted so desperately to know what became of Mama. How life treated her after Joe Dee and I had to go."

"I guess you could say your mom wasn't a strong woman, able to survive the hard knocks of life. Some can and some can't. And with two small children to raise, it was more than she could bear up to." Ida's face showed pity.

"I know."

"Just don't, my child, hold it against your mama. She loved you. I know it for a fact Just remember her that way and be glad that you found out."

Persia got up to leave. "Thank you, Ida, for sharing. You've given me a chapter of my life that was missing. God bless you." Persia extended her hand to Ida's. "You're a sweet lady."

Outside, she started the car for the drive back to the City. Now, if she could only locate Joe Dee

* * * *   * * * *   * * * *

Time between Christmas and Easter seemed jet-propelled. With all the details of property and school, Persia grew more stressed each day. The decision to donate Claremont and its gardens and art to the city of Pittsburgh came with a struggle. Would Bebe and Mumsy approve if they knew? The place presented far too many problems for one, especially one with so little experience at business and management. Besides, the place did nothing but send her into a state of depression with all its memories. She needed to see new faces, make new friends, even travel when school permitted.

By the end of April, her decision was sealed. With Maud already living in Missouri near her brother, it made sense to go through with her plans. Yes, she would sell most of the Pittsburgh property and donate the house and furnishings to the city. She'd finish the semester at the University, then move away—to where, she had no idea. But first a trip to South Carolina. She'd promised Reid Morgan for over a year; it was time to make good on her word. In May when school was out for the summer, the trip would be first on her agenda. A promise made is a promise kept—by golly, she'd go.

CHAPTER 32

The winter in Louisville was raw; cold winds with some snow, but by the first of April, signs of spring jumped up everywhere. Yet, in spite of the seasonal beauty, Joe Hartsong's apprehension grew by the day. Would High Pockets perform in the Derby, or react like an unpredictable toddler dead set on getting his way?

Recently, the colt had run better—when the mood hit him—but at any sound or whim he'd rear, twist, even whinny, the same behavior he'd exhibited at the Oaklawn race! Finally, during that race, with Joe's patience, the horse responded to dash forward as astutely as a champion to finish behind five lengths. Claudia, on hearing it, flew into despair and had called daily since February to check. "Does my horse have any chance at success?" she'd asked repeatedly. To which both Dan and Joe always offered encouragement, but both secretly wondered if High Pockets had any talent on the racetrack!

"Got a minute?" Dan yelled to Joe one morning after High Pockets's gallop session.

"Be right there," Joe yelled back, somewhat encouraged. The horse had followed instructions and finished well for a change.

"Claudia called again," Dan began. "She's having second thoughts about High Pockets and the Derby. I can tell from her voice that she's depressed."

"She can't do that; too late," Joe gasped. "I thought that once—"

"She thinks it's too risky… unpredictable," Dan added and shook his head in disgust. "How did he do this morning?"

"Better'n usual," Joe blurted, not willing to forfeit his chances at becoming a jockey—in the Derby of all races. "What did you tell her?"

"To start with, a Derby contender must be nominated and must have racked up a substantial purse," Dan informed. "Unless some horse is scratched, there's little chance anyway."

For the next few minutes, they knocked about one option after another. "Let's wait a couple of days. She may change her mind," Joe suggested before he got up to leave. It was eleven. The food vendors at the grandstand would open in thirty minutes. If he felt hungry, he'd eat; recently his appetite was next to nothing… too much stress, he told himself on his way to his room. "Nothing's gone right lately."

Still agonizing that evening over Claudia's uncertainty, he picked up the telephone to place a call to her. If he could convince her that the horse could run—and he knew High Pockets could run—but getting him to do it—well, that was something else—she might just change her thinking and relent. Besides, details were already in place for the Derby, and any attempt to change them was out of his control.

He punched in the area code, then hesitated. "Dang!" he muttered and laid the phone on the table as another fear surfaced. Claudia might hire another jockey—somebody more experienced. Yep, in her distraught state, she might just do it. He jumped up, popped on his boots, and headed for the stable. "Horses have plenty of sense," Mr. Murphy back in Oklahoma always said "They'll listen to you if they know you, trust you. They like that one-on-one relationship." Surely, High Pockets knew his voice by now, touch, too. No question about it, Joe told himself. "But why won't he respond to me?" Joe stepped to the horse's head with a gentle rub across the nose. "Good boy," he whispered and placed his own cheek next to that of the horse. "We're a team. You're my boy, aren't you? We have some work to do, though. Understand, big boy?"

The horse nudged Joe's arm as Joe continued to speak. "We're in this together. Let's show 'em what we can do, okay? Okay, big boy?"

Again, High Pockets lowered his head in submission and nudged Joe's chest. "They're saying we're failures, that we can't do that racetrack out there. Let's show 'em." Joe knelt to check High Pocket's leg joints. Noticing that the right one was swollen, he began to massage it. "Does that feel better, boy? Does it make you more comfortable, uh, boy?"

"Learn to communicate," he remembered from an article he'd read on horse training, but whether it would work with High Pockets was another question.

* * * * * * * * * *

The telephone rang the next evening. Claudia again.

"Got a minute," was her usual greeting. Her voice sounded subdued. "I've been thinking, Joe."

Joe frowned fearfully. What was she up to this time?

"I've meant to call you," Joe interrupted. "Been working overtime with your horse. Giving 'im plenty of attention."

"Dan says it's too late to withdraw High Pockets from the Derby. Says he can qualify barely, especially if another horse scratches. He advises me to go forward with it, take my chances. Says it's the name of the game, anyway. Always surprises in racin'."

"He's right." Suddenly, his heart tumbled, then seemed to stop. Had Dan talked some sense into her?

"Do you think a more accomplished jockey might help... might be the solution?"

"Th—that's up to you, Claudia. I sure..." The feared blow had come with vengeance! Sweat popped out on his brow. His hands trembled!

"I realize you know my horse better'n anyone," she said. "That was my reason for all this preparation. But I can't lose money on the horse, Joe. Just can't. I've spent too much already."

A spike went straight through him. He couldn't have felt worse. "You know what is best, Claudia. Tell me truthfully how you feel. If another jockey is what you want—" His voice cracked. To think that his one big break to ride in the Derby had suddenly dwindled to nothing! "You decide and let me know," was all he said before he disconnected the call and cried like a baby!

* * * *   * * * *   * * * *

Disturbed and devastated, Joe avoided everyone for days; he could hardly speak without breaking into tears—something he considered himself too hardened for. He'd lived through many disappointments, but this took the prize! Even Dan seemed distant, aloof; perhaps, he was already busy at hiring another jockey. It was anyone's guess, but whatever was underway, Joe felt in no mood to discuss it. Yet, as his habit was, he continued to slip into High Pockets's stall each night for a few quiet minutes. His love of horses had carried him through many an ordeal at the Murphy's back in Oklahoma, had helped to take his sadness away. Now it was the calm petting and soft talk to High Pockets that relaxed him more than anything. Whether he ever raced the horse again or not didn't constrain his deep admiration; High Pockets was a good horse. He'd bet on 'im any day, and the respect he had for him wouldn't be measured by a single race.

* * * *   * * * *   * * * *

A week passed uneventfully.

"Have you spoken to the valet about your silks? Do they need pressing?" It was Dan one morning in early May as Joe stood and watched a hot air balloon go up. The two-week annual Derby's Festival was underway, and the city was in a party mood.

"What?" Joe, stunned, turned to face him.

"Claudia didn't call you? She's here in town and wants to go over plans."

"What plans?"

"You're to be her jockey."

"You're kiddin'." His jaw dropped. "Me? I thought she'd changed her mind."

"Nope. She'll arrive out here any minute now, but told me last night that you're the one. Where were you?"

Joe didn't answer. He hadn't told Dan about his evening sessions with High Pockets. No point in it "The odds are against us, I'm sure," Joe said, still stunned. "But I know one thing; I'm gonna give it my all. It'll be the ride of my life even if we come up short. Are you sure she wants me?"

"Sure," Dan responded emphatically.

"Never thought I'd see the day. Even if High Pockets gets out on the track and lies down, I can say I've raced in the Derby." He chuckled with every ounce of his small body.

"You know what they say," Dan began. "It's all in the jockey's hands and voice that motivates the horse to perform, do his best. Just go out there and show your stuff." Dan advised and turned to go.

Joe didn't answer. He knew he'd prepared High Pockets, worked with 'im like crazy for the last two weeks. Now, it was up to fate, he told himself, still unable to realize his luck.

"Guess you're ready for action," Claudia said when she arrived that morning. Her blue eyes danced with enthusiasm. "This is the race to win," she said. "Let's put it over."

"Changed your mind," Joe replied. "I hope I won't disappoint you. It's a big challenge, you know. Very big. High Pockets can behave strangely at times, downright crazy, but I know he can run," Joe said as they strolled toward the grandstand for coffee. "I *know* your horse, Claudia."

"I've decided to let it be, go with the flow. If he flubs, he flubs. I'm weary of it," Claudia confessed and seemed content with her decision, whatever it might result in.

May 7th arrived with fanfare—Derby Day! Crowds, hats, horses and mint juleps! The place teemed with visitors and spectators, music and food! Among all the others, rumor had it that a nice thoroughbred three-year-old colt named Ginny Fizz was the horse to beat. Spectators craned, pushed, and shoved to see Ginny Fizz! "Good gosh," Joe muttered. "Never saw such commotion in my life. Guess me and High Pockets don't stand a chance. Sure is scary." Reporters, television cameras, and sportscasters from all over wanted a peek at Ginny Fizz. "If I could only back out now…"

"But nothing worthwhile comes without a struggle," he remembered Chub back in California had said.

Claudia and Roslynn arrived with cheers and hugs. Roslynn appeared to have grown three inches… a pretty little thing, too. "What are the odds, Joe?" she blurted acting as if she understood the racing business.

"Odds? 9-1, they tell me. We sure can't get our hopes up. High Pockets will get the 20th post, too, which puts us at a disadvantage—far out on the track."

Claudia's expression dropped. She shook her head. "Terrible," she mumbled, almost in tears. "This is gonna be one big heartbreak. I may not be able to watch it."

The visit ended and Joe again slipped into High Pockets's stall. The groom would arrive any minute to bathe and fancy the colt up. The backside was quiet; the preparations crew hadn't begun. Actually, there were to be seven races; the Derby the last.

"Good boy," Joe again whispered when he was alone with High Pockets. "Today is our day to run in this big race. They think we can't do it. The horse nudged Joe's arm as if he understood. "Please come through for me, boy. This has been a long, hard road for me—and you. Let's show 'em. Okay?" Joe pressed his cheek against High Pockets's face and slipped away into the morning air. His silks were surely ready and hanging in the jockeys' quarters. He had already weighed in at 109 pounds, 5 ounces with a height of 5 feet 3 inches, all necessary for the handicapping process.

By the time the Derby was to begin, Joe was dressed in his bright blue silks, boots as shiny as new money, and cap that covered most of his tawny hair. Trying to concentrate on the task ahead, he sat to himself in the jockeys' quarters and noticed other scheduled jockeys as they played cards, read the paper, or napped. How, he wondered, could they remain calm? Only minutes remained until they'd go down to the paddock to saddle up.

At the backside, Dan, Claudia, and Roslynn began the traditional "walk," the stroll from the stables to the paddock. Spectators, with programs in hand, crowded the fence for a close-up view of their choices. Handicappers, thoroughly grounded in the racing stats of each horse, circulated through the crowd while Joe literally bit his nails. Would his mount run or balk? Would he win or lose?

After a few minutes in the paddock, the bugler sounded and the paddock judge yelled, "Riders up." Joe pulled himself into the saddle, his short legs tight against High Pockets's shoulders. The prepost parade began as an enormous crowd watched, cheered, and threw kisses! High Pockets pranced like a champion! "Good boy," Joe whispered when they finally reached the gate. Now, for the real test. Joe's heart raced; his muscles tightened. "Let go," he told himself. "Let the nerves go. Give your all. Work with your horse. Concentrate. Give it two minutes of spine and grit." The bell rang and the call, "They're off," sounded. Joe leaned forward for the race of his life! Sink or swim, he was racing in the Derby!

CHAPTER 33

At the Baggage Claim in Charleston that early May morning, Persia looked into Reid Morgan's eyes, dark and full of casual friendliness. "I finally made it," she greeted, determined to let go and relax during her visit. After months of classes and business transactions—the donation of Claremont and Claire's art collection to the city, she felt tired, stressed, and sad, but realized it all went exactly according to her mother's liking. The spacious house with its ornate gardens seemed ideal for a gallery, yet the process had not gone without much introspection and emotional strain. To think of the times she'd seen her mother stop her activities to admire one of her paintings, or the times she'd seen Maud dust the treasured frames brought tears to her eyes.

"Welcome to Charleston. Flight okay?" the tall, nicely dressed scientist greeted.

"Okay." She pointed to her bag as the carousel brought it around. "That one," she said as he grabbed it.

Reid was a bigger man than she remembered from the reception in

Beaufort. Handsome, too; prominent jaw line, dark wavy hair that fell over the brow on one side and gorgeous eyes that exuded intelligence. "Bet you're hungry," he said as they headed toward the car.

"A little, yes, something light, a salad, maybe."

"I know just the place; a garden café down near the water's edge." He threw her bag in the back seat and opened the car door. "You're gonna love Charleston. After lunch, we'll spin around town to give you a tour. See what you think." He turned toward her and winked. "And your hotel overlooks the harbor. A view you won't soon forget."

"And your lab? I'm anxious to see that notorious blue-blooded crab." She giggled. "Must be something—some aristocratic varmint of sorts... that blue blood." She giggled slightly, later realizing he must think her terribly dumb.

"Oh, as a matter of fact, the horseshoe crab *is* quite numerous here... water organisms they are. They have gills like fish. You'll see."

"The data you sent sure helped with my paper. Impressed my tutor, too. Did I tell you that I made an A?" She grinned. "I wouldn't have known where to start without it. Science isn't my best subject."

"Good for you. Glad I helped."

After lunch at a quaint little restaurant among arbors of jasmine and beds of roses, Reid insisted they look around. "Is this your first trip here?" he asked.

"Yes, and I hope I'm not hindering you from your work," she said as he started the motor.

"No way. I work on my own. Don't account to anyone except with test results. Dr. Wilson, my department head, leaves it to me. I turn out the tests, share the results, and the man is quite happy." He grinned, showing slight dimples and pearly white teeth.

He drove slowly down King Street and later around the shoreline toward the harbor at the junction of Ashley and Cooper Rivers. "The city has wonderful water sports, kayaking, deep-sea fishing, and for sure you need to take a sunset tour of the harbor aboard a schooner. It's beautiful with seagulls soaring overhead and sea breezes in your face." Again, he smiled proudly. "Some life, Persia. I love it here. I may just settle here for good."

"You like the ocean, I assume."

"Love it. After a tiresome day's work, I can get out on the water and become a new person within minutes."

"And look at all the palmetto trees," Persia added. "I guess that's what they are."

"Yes, people here garden a lot. You notice their lawns—always manicured perfectly."

"I've noticed already."

"If time permits, I have another place that I want you to see, Camden. It's a quaint little town. My family winters in Camden each year and have for as long as I can remember. You'll fall in love with it," he said as he drove.

"You're from the North I assume."

"Rhode Island." He didn't elaborate. "Camden's an old polo town. Do you like horses?" He glanced toward her with a grin.

"Polo in South Carolina? I'm surprised."

"Oh, sure. In fact, they have the annual Colonial Cup in Camden, nice race track, too. You'll see. Yep, Camden is horse country."

She realized immediately that he was determined to take her to Camden. "Sounds nice, but for now, let's go see your lab."

"That we shall do. I guess I get carried away at the idea of horseback riding." He chuckled. "Women and horses always dumbfound me."

"Remember I came here to see that little crab… and you, too, of course."

"You'd better say that." He winked obviously anxious to show her around.

She flipped her hair to one side flirtatiously and said, "Yes, the two of you. But that little creature surely has raised my curiosity. And I can tell, you're a converted Southerner, already."

He soon pulled into the parking lot and directed her through a complex of buildings that adjoined a hospital. "This is it," he said as they entered a work space filled with all kinds of scientific equipment, most of which she'd never seen.

"This is Connie," he said. "My lab assistant. Persia Plemons of Pittsburgh." Connie glanced up but soon continued her work.

Reid stepped to the freezer and took out a small test tube. "See, nothing to it. Just blood."

"Blue for sure, and the crabs? Do you have any here?"

"Sure. Over here. Come take a look." He motioned to a tank on the other side of the room.

Persia followed and peeped to see six horseshoe crabs lying docile in a layer of water. "My gosh, they really do resemble a horseshoe, don't they?"

"Guess that's how they got their name, reckon? Funny little creatures, aren't they?" He picked one up for her to get a better look.

"You really don't hurt them, do you?"

"They hardly know they've had a visit here," he assured her with a reassuring expression and returned the crab to the tank. "We draw a small portion of blood and return them to the sea."

An hour passed with questions and explanations as she carefully scrutinized the place. Impressed, she hardly noticed how fast the time flew. Perhaps a scientific career wasn't out of the question for her; she'd learned to appreciate the analytical and thorough study that it required.

Now, if he insisted, she'd go to Camden for a more leisurely aspect of her visit. Why not? School was out and the entire summer was ahead.

* * * *   * * * *   * * * *

Camden was a dream, and his family's guest house suited her to a T. A back window afforded a great view; a riding trail that ran along a tree-lined street. Reid's knowledge of horses astounded her, too. He even owned one named Marky, which met all the qualifications of a fine specimen.

"Kids here learn to ride young," he explained at the stables. "And I must introduce you to Kirkwood Lane where some of the finest homes are. It'll blow your mind, but first let's hitch up and go for a ride."

"Me, ride? You gotta be kidding. I know absolutely nothing about horses."

"I'll show you. There's nothing to it. First, relax. Make 'im think you know what you're doing," he advised handing her the reins.

"Ready as I'll ever get," she grunted, too nervous for words. What if the darn horse takes off in a tear, or worse, throws me head-first into the dirt? she thought, trembling terribly.

* * * * * * * * * * * *

Time in Camden passed faster than a March snowstorm, and yes, by some streak of luck, she stayed in the saddle more than once. In addition to dinner at romantic cafes, hikes into the countryside, and brief visits with friends he'd made over the years, the week flew. Needless to say, South Carolina grew on her, and so did Reid. When might she ever see him again? His polite and caring manner was more than she'd expected. But did he have a girlfriend? Or worse still, a wife? Why had he not so much as asked to kiss her? Did he consider her too young and inexperienced? She'd guess him at least twenty-five. Why had she suddenly begun to crave more from him than mere sightseeing and adventure? But the trip, she reminded herself, was in no way supposed to hold romantic endeavors… merely a casual trip south to see a darn horseshoe crab! She laughed out loud and galloped away down the shady trail.

* * * * * * * * * * * *

Saturday came sunny and bright. Reid knocked on her door early and looked ravishing in a white sport shirt and khaki slacks… so that every muscle showed through. One hunk of a guy if you ask me, she thought, scrutinizing him carefully.

"Let's go for a ride before breakfast," he said. "Want to?" Enthusiasm was written all over his face.

"Sure, but give me a minute."

"Why don't I go for some Danish while you dress. We'll eat after the ride. Okay?"

"Some coffee, please. A mocha. I can heat it in the microwave when we're ready."

She dressed quickly and arranged her long hair into an upsweep, then applied plenty of sunscreen. The South Carolina sun was hot.

"Just thought of something," he said later with a grin. "This is Kentucky Derby Day. Wanna watch it this afternoon?"

"Be fine. I'd forgotten."

"Forgotten the Derby! Land's sakes, gal. How could you? It's one big event... one of the finest, by far. I wouldn't dare miss it."

"You've gone to Louisville to see it, I assume."

"Five times already and would have gone this year but had a paper to prepare for a meeting in two weeks. You haven't?"

"I haven't, but not for any good reason. Guess I've never taken the time." She tucked her head embarrassed, of all things.

"You must go sometime. It's the big party in that part of the country."

"Look, you realize I'll go home tomorrow morning. I can't thank you enough for a nice visit, but I feel as though I'm taking too much of your time." Somehow, she felt totally inadequate. When had she ever taken up horse racing?

"Taking my time? Come off it. A respite from work with a gorgeous woman? How crazy do you think I am?" He reached for her hand. "I feel like I know you already, Persia. You give me a chance to do something besides look at test tubes."

Neither spoke for a moment She hoped he'd lean forward and kiss her. She needed to know he approved of her.

"Please say you'll come again. I don't meet many women so interesting *and* pretty." He sidled up to her and drew her to him passionately. "I'll miss you when you leave. Really, I will."

"You can't be serious."

"Why wouldn't I be?"

She didn't answer.

* * * * * * * * *

The morning passed, and by late afternoon, they returned to his family's homestead to watch the Derby on TV. Already an enormous crowd; people mixing and mingling in boisterous confusion jammed the spacious grandstand. Beautiful horses and gorgeous women in big hats, some sipping what she assumed was mint juleps, each stylish and crowding closer to the rail for a better view of the soon-to-be race. A reporter gave stats of the horses and events as they occurred. A three-year-old colt named Ginny Fizz was favored to win, he announced.

"Which is your pick?" she asked, watching the horses go into the paddock.

"Ginny Fizz for sure. From all reports, he's the colt of the year. Great stats. He comes from a farm in Virginia."

"Interesting," she mumbled, not really into the race. From her point of view, it was merely a popular sporting event. If she knew more about horses, she'd probably share his enthusiasm. One fact was clear; horse racing was a wealthy man's sport. Reid Morgan's family had money, old money and lots of it. The race was about to begin, and he seemed totally in awe of the line-up. "Some beautiful horse," she said as the excitement grew and Ginny Fizz led the parade.

"I'll say," he replied, not taking his eyes off the set.

CHAPTER 34

The bell rang and the gate opened! The Derby was on! Reid Morgan edged up on his chair to turn up the volume on the TV. Ginny Fizz, the horse expected to win, broke a clean lead as the cheering crowd roared. "Watch that baby go," Reid shouted, obviously thrilled and totally absorbed, just as Pearly Waters, a number seven, edged in close to the rail. High Pockets, far out, lagged at the first turn as Ginny Fizz, with extended stride, kept the lead.

Spectators, out of town celebrities, locals, even foreigners cheered, whistled, and yelled as prized thoroughbreds from all over showed their stuff! And the sportscaster almost dropped the microphone when Pearly Waters edged ahead of Ginny Fizz and High Pockets, number twenty, began to weave toward the rail.

"My gosh, what's going on?" Reid blurted when Ginny Fizz lagged so that Pearly Waters took the lead.

Persia grunted slightly, fascinated by it all—totally amused at Reid's enthusiasm, especially when Kindly Fables pulled forward and High Pockets wedged between Pearly Waters and Kindly Fables.

"That jockey'd better pull some magic if he wants Ginny Fizz to win," Reid mumbled, his expression sour. Just then, Pearly Waters edged forward as Kindly Fables lagged and almost stumbled. High Pockets, now at the rail, evened up with Pearly Waters and the two ran neck and neck until Pearly Waters edged ahead, but Ginny Fizz overtook him. The crowd roared to see the favorite ahead.

In a moment's notice, High Pockets's jockey tapped the colt's rump and leaned into his ear, obviously prodding him on, as the colt dashed— ears pinned back and nostrils flared—a full stride ahead. But not for long. Kindly Fables, now close on, pushing and panting, pulled into the lead. Again, the crowd cheered! Joe Hartsong, High Pockets's jockey, leaned forward again. The finish line was in sight. Suddenly, High Pockets dashed forward and over the line. Pearly Waters, then Kindly Fables.

"Hell's bells," Reid yelled. "What happened? I can't believe this! What happened to Ginny Fizz." His face turned a glowing red.

Joe Hartsong, on number twenty, had managed the impossible. With his careful maneuvering and steady hand, he had won the famous Derby! Pearly Waters placed, and Kindly Fables showed.

"My gosh, I still can't believe this!" Reid fussed. That number twenty came from nowhere to win over Ginny Fizz. Some upset, if you ask me." He shook his head in disgust. "You never can predict these races. Guess that's why they keep us watching. Somebody made a pocketful of money… the odds."

The winner's circle soon filled with the McClish clan. Reporters eager to interview the jockey pushed in to ask how Hartsong managed the upset. Joe, in his bright blue silks and racing boots, sat in the saddle with glee written all over his young face!

"How'd you pull it off?" one reporter asked. "Some upset, I'd say."

"I knew my horse. I asked 'im to run for me, and he did," Joe replied and squared his shoulders proudly.

"What do you attribute this win to, Mrs. McClish?" another reporter asked Claudia.

"Good trainer, good jockey. I knew if anyone could get it out of my horse, Joe Hartsong could, and he did." She beamed with success written all over her face! "Tremendous effort on his part. He's the best."

At the name *Hartsong*, Persia jumped from her chair wide-eyed and gasping! "Who is the jockey? What is his name?"

"*Hartsong*. Joe Hartsong, I think they said. Never heard of him, have you?"

Hartsong? Are you sure? I know someone by that name," she stammered, almost not getting it out. "A relative. Where did they say he's from?"

"I didn't get it. Let's see if they tell."

"I think I may know him," Persia repeated, her heart racing, her muscles tight!

"You say you think you know him?" Reid asked and turned the volume down. "He's a relative. My gosh, what a coincidence."

"Yes, but how the kid ever got to become a jockey, I'm not sure. Am I hearing things or what? There has to be a mistake."

"Somebody sure made a ton of money on those odds," Reid repeated matter-of-factly. "Good race, though. I still can't believe the outcome... what happened to Ginny Fizz." His expression fell.

Persia's thoughts had already passed the race. "You have a telephone here?" she asked. "I'll pay you for a long distance charge. I want to check on that jockey. See if I'm nuts or what." She managed a giggle. "This can't be true."

"No sweat, help yourself."

Persia stepped to the phone and placed a call to Louisville. "Information, please. Churchill Downs."

The operator gave the number and she dialed.

"May I help you?" a voice at the other end said.

"Do you have the number for Joe Hartsong, the jockey who rode the winner today? I'd like to congratulate him," she said in her most polite manner.

"Sorry, ma'am. I can't help you with that. You might contact the horse's owner or trainer." Then a click.

"No luck," she mumbled, disappointed, and returned to her chair. Guess I should've known they'd respect his privacy.

* * * * * * * * *

At the airport the next morning, Reid gave her a brush on the cheek and said, "Please come again. You've given me a full week's rest from work and more fun than you'll ever know. Don't wait so long next time." He grinned so that his full lips parted seductively as he pulled her to him. "I'll miss you."

"The pleasure was all mine, and guess what? I can now say that I can ride a horse." She squeezed his arm with a giggle. "You've been a great host, Reid. I loved every minute of it." She pulled away to check in. "See ya," she yelled as she entered the airport, determined to try another phone call to the jockeys' quarters this time. Perhaps someone could direct her to Joe Dee. But it was Sunday. Darn! Why did she have to wait another day?

CHAPTER 35

WALKING DOWN THE LONG corridor toward the American Airlines gate, she spotted another telephone, determined to try another call to Louisville.

"Churchill Downs," a voice answered.

"I'm trying to connect with Joe Hartsong, the jockey who rode the winner yesterday. Could you tell me where he's from or how I might locate him? I didn't get the horse's owner's name."

"Claudia McClish. California, ma'am," the voice replied and abruptly hung up.

"Darn," she blurted, aggravated, and rushed toward the gate when she heard her flight announced. "California? Claudia McClish? But where in California?"

* * * *   * * * *   * * * *

The flight into Pittsburgh seemed eons long. To think she'd come so close to connecting with Joe Dee—or was the jockey not Joe at all? Same names do occur. As yet, she'd never heard of anyone named

Persia—Claire's idea, definitely not hers, but Jessie, plenty of those, she mused, still absorbed in the Derby.

At Claremont, she unlocked the door and entered. By contract with the city, she'd have to move out by July 1st. Stressed at the idea and her disappointment at not reaching that jockey—whoever he was—she set her bag down in the library to think. "Claudia McClish," she muttered, and anxiously ran her palm across her brow. *How might I reach her? Directory Assistance*, she decided, but to what city? She reached for the phone, then put it down again.

"Churchill Downs," a voice repeated much as the first call when she placed another call to the backside.

"Sir, I'm desperately trying to connect with Joe Hartsong… he's my brother, sir, and I haven't seen 'im in years. Please help me," she sobbed into the telephone. "Or I—I think, I think he's my brother."

"Look," the voice began. "Call Rick Stubblefield at the backside. Joe has worked with Rick. He might help you… put you onto 'im. That'd be my suggestion."

"At the track, you mean?"

"Yeah, Rick works here. If anyone knows, he would. That is, besides Claudia McClish. Try 'im."

Her chest tightened; her heart raced. A knot seemed to choke off her breath. "Do you have the extension for Rick Stubblefield?"

"Try extension 830."

She quickly hung up and redialed. "830, please," she muttered nervously into the phone, but no answer. She threw the phone down and angrily paced the floor.

* * * *   * * * *   * * * *

Monday morning, too distraught to unpack, she again paced the long corridor to the kitchen. Within weeks, the city planned to send movers to start removing furnishings from the house. "Movers," she groaned. "They'll expect me out of here. But to where? Why did I act so hastily, just at the time when I may have seen my brother win the Kentucky Derby, the Run for the Roses of all things, or was it really my brother? Probably just another illusion. No way she'd be up to a decision on relocation with knowledge that he might be alive and well in California.

She picked up the telephone again for another try to Louisville. Trembling uncontrollably, she almost dropped the phone when someone answered. A male, it was. The voice was young-sounding, too, and vibrant.

"Are you the jockey who rode the winner in the Derby yesterday?" she inquired, fearful that he'd hang up and refuse to speak.

"Joe Hartsong, ma'am. How can I help you?"

"Do you have a sister—a sister named *Jessie*? Her voice cracked with emotion as tears spilled over her hand and into the phone.

"Used to. Barely remember her, though, uh."

"Joe, this is your sister, Jessie," she sobbed.

"You must have the wrong number, Miss."

"No, I saw the Derby, and when they introduced you as Joe Hartsong, I almost flipped. You have to be Joe Dee, my brother. I've prayed to find you for so long. Please say you remember me."

"Where are you? Are you sure you have the right number?" The young male seemed stunned, confused.

"You don't remember a sister? A sister back in Oklahoma?"

"Well, I kinda do. I remember Duncan, Oklahoma. Do you live in Duncan?"

"No, we lived in Carlisle. Remember the trailer court and the little brook where you looked for frogs?" Her voice was clearer now. "I made your oatmeal each morning before the school bus ran. Remember how I'd cry when I missed it?"

"My gosh, I never dreamed I'd—"

"You do remember?"

"Jessie, is it really you... Where are you? When can I—?"

"Can you meet me in Oklahoma City at the airport soon? I can fly down any time."

"You bet I can, Jessie. It's been too long."

"Tomorrow?" she pleaded ecstatically.

"Better make it Tuesday. Claudia, she's the owner of the horse I rode. She's still here, Jessie, a terrific lady... really been nice to me." His voice had a boyish quality to it. Say, could we ride down to Carlisle and check on Mama? I can't believe this... that it's really you."

Persia froze. Mama's dead. How would she break the news—get it across how Mama had undergone so much pain, loss of her children, her cancer, life in general? Tears spilled again as they said goodbye. Years and much yearning had passed since the two of them rode hand in hand away from their simple life in Oklahoma, and to think they were about to finally reunite! "A dream, this is a dream," she kept mumbling. "I've finally found 'im... my little brother."

* * * * * * * * * *

Waiting for his arrival on Tuesday at the Oklahoma City airport was like waiting to see what Santa left under the Christmas tree. Would he recognize the name change from *Jessie* to *Persia*?

241

At ten thirty that morning, his flight was to arrive, and every cell in her body tensed as taut as a yoyo's string. Nervously, she glanced at her watch—twelve minutes to go.

At the baggage claim a few minutes later, she thought she saw him… a neatly dressed teen who paced beside the luggage carousel. A band of freckles showed across the nose. The blond hair, a bit darker now with some brown in it, was neatly combed to the side. His body, though small of frame, showed muscles through his shirt as though he'd pumped iron.

"Pardon me," she squealed finally reaching him. "Are you Joe Dee Hartsong, the jockey?"

"Yes," he replied and straightened his shoulders. "You must be Jessie." He grabbed her into a bear hug.

"Yes," she whispered with outstretched arms. "I am. Finally, it's you, Joe Dee. I've waited so long… so, so long to find you, hear your voice again."

For several minutes, neither spoke as the carousel with his bag made round after round.

"Let's go for lunch and catch up on the years," Persia suggested and realized she had some explaining to do; the Plemons name, her adoptive parents both now deceased, and Mama's demise.

"Tell me," she said as they entered the restaurant for lunch. "How did you pull off that win at the Derby Saturday? That was some race."

"It's a long story, sis, but I do have one favor to ask of you. After we check on Carlisle and Mama, could we drive over to Duncan?" His face reflected concern.

"Why Duncan?"

"I think I owe Mr. Murphy an apology."

"Mr. Murphy. Who's Mr. Murphy?"

"He was my foster dad at the time, and he bought me a horse that I named *Rusty*. When I came up with two F's on my report card, he sold Rusty. It liked to killed me, too."

"Sold 'im? Why, for Heaven's sake?"

"Yeah, one day while I was at school. He thought I was spending too much time with my horse. I failed two subjects. I ran away. Thought he was a mean old dude. You know how kids think sometimes."

"Guess so." Persia didn't quite understand, but understood how disappointments hurt.

"But you know what? I think he was trying to make something outta me." Joe's eyes misted. "I wanna go tell 'im I'm sorry." He wiped his face and managed a grin. "He might be sorta proud of me after the Derby. Reckon?"

"Sure, we'll go. Foster parents did a lot for us, Joe. Of course, we didn't realize it at the time. Do kids ever?" She reached for his hand and squeezed it. "But you know, those hardships didn't hurt us. Just look, somehow we've managed to do okay for ourselves. Don't ya think?" She hugged him again, vowing never to lose him again!

CPSIA information can be obtained at www.ICGtesting.com
Printed in the USA
240748LV00001B/6/P

9 781456 727543